WAIT FOR ALWAYS

WAIT FOR ALWAYS

K.A. LINDE

For every reader who chose the "wrong guy" in the love triangle and sent me emails cursing my name.

This one is for you.

ALSO BY K. A. LINDE

COASTAL CHRONICLES

Hold the Forevers

At First Hate

Second to None

Wait for Always

Wait for Always
Copyright © 2023 by K.A. Linde
All rights reserved.

Visit my website at
www.kalinde.com

Cover Designer: Staci Hart,
www.stacihartnovels.com
Photography: Michelle Lancaster,
www.michellelancaster.com
Editor: Unforeseen Editing,
www.unforeseenediting.com

No part of this book may be reproduced or transmitted in any form or by any means, electronic or mechanical, including photocopying, recording, or by any information storage and retrieval system without the written permission of the author, except for the use of brief quotations in a book review.

This book is a work of fiction. Names, characters, places, and incidents either are products of the author's imagination or are used fictitiously. Any resemblance to actual persons, living or dead, events, or locales is entirely coincidental.

ISBN-13: 978-1948427722

PART I

1

SAVANNAH
PRESENT

The only available parking spot was in front of the fire hydrant.

I narrowed my eyes in exasperation. Of course, on the day that I had to deal with this, there wasn't going to be a single spot in downtown Savannah. This morning was an uncharacteristic eighty degrees and ninety percent humidity in *March*, and I had a *meeting* to get to after this.

But no ... my dick ex needed me to get my shit out of his house today, or he was going to—quote—"chuck it out the window." It didn't matter that I'd been asking to come over to get my stuff for weeks. He'd refused at every turn. So, while I knew jumping at the first chance he gave me was playing exactly into his hand, I might never get my favorite cardigan back if I didn't.

"Bastard," I muttered under my breath.

I parallel parked in front of the fire hydrant,

K.A. LINDE

prayed that I wouldn't get a ticket, then popped the door on my BMW, and rushed to the sidewalk. My heels clicked noisily as I stormed up the front walk of the dilapidated house. Mark had inherited it from his great uncle and didn't have the liquid assets to keep it in adequate shape despite or because of his flagrant use of daddy's money in everything else in his life. The number of red flags I'd ignored climbed ever higher.

I rang the doorbell and tapped my foot. Mark had always hated that. So now, I did it with relish while I waited.

No one came to the door though, and my long, straight brown hair was beginning to curl at the end. I rang again, knowing Mark hated that too.

"Christ, Amelia," Mark snapped as he wrenched the door open. "So impatient."

Seven months, nine days, and about fourteen hours—that was exactly how long I'd wasted my time with Mark Armstrong.

"Can I have my stuff?" I asked, not keeping the irritation out of my voice.

I couldn't even reach for my pageant smile. With the snarl I could barely contain on my lips, no one would ever know that I'd won Miss Georgia

"Don't want to come in and have a drink?" he asked, leaning against the doorframe.

He was exactly my type—tall, dark, and handsome with daddy's money and an old Savannah surname

Wait for Always

that matched mine. I'd excused a lot of behavior for how well we should have fit together.

"I just want my stuff. Let's not do this today."

His smile lit up at my rude behavior. "Come on, pageant queen. Give me a smile."

I couldn't manage it. I just crossed my arms. "Mark."

"Fine, fine," he grumbled. "Jesus, never could take a joke."

A joke. Right.

He kicked a box across the threshold. Actually kicked it.

I reached down and looked through the contents. Of course, my cardigan wasn't in there. "Where's my cardigan? The Taylor Swift one."

"Fuck if I know."

The same old panic took over me at the anger in his voice. Who knew how close he was to letting out that anger on me? I could never quite tell. Still, I refused to back down.

"You know that's my favorite. I came, just like you wanted me to, so I could get it back."

"It's not my fault that you leave your shit everywhere."

"Fine. I'll look for it myself." I took a half-step toward the house, ready to barrel him down and find that damn cardigan when he burst into laughter.

"Oh, your face. Man, Amelia, you should see yourself. Here's your fucking cardigan."

He reached into the room and tossed it at me. It hit me in the face, and I caught it, trying to suppress my revulsion that I'd ever dated someone this mercilessly cruel. It had taken me a long time to see this in him. Everyone who knew him liked him. No one suspected that how he was in public wasn't who he was in private. And I'd finally gotten tired of it all. Tired of no one believing me and everyone thinking I was crazy for leaving him. At least I knew well enough not to provoke him any further.

"Thanks, Mark," I said, dropping the cardi into the box and hefting it into my arms.

"You sure you don't want to come in?" He shot me a licentious smile.

"I'm quite sure," I forced out, taking a step back.

His smile fell, and irritation flared in his eyes. "I'm over here, doing you a huge favor. I got all of your stuff together. I made myself available for you. And you can't even do me the decency of coming inside?"

I was never going into that house again if I could help it.

"What? Too good for me now? Who else are you going to find that's going to want you?"

I said nothing. Nothing that I wanted to say would be productive. I'd heard that from him before. I'd heard it enough to not know up from down. But even if no one else ever wanted me again, I didn't want *him*.

Better yet, I was getting the hell out of Savannah soon enough if all went to plan.

Wait for Always

"Unless you're just running back to Ash," Mark said.

I winced.

I shouldn't have, but I did.

When we'd first gotten together, I'd confessed everything to him. How I'd loved Ash Talmadge my entire life while he loved someone else. And how when I finally—*finally*—had my chance, we'd fucked it all up.

Mark knew enough to be dangerous. Enough to make it so that I'd barely seen Ash for the seven months Mark and I had dated. And when we had run into Ash, Mark's jealousy had run so hot that I knew better than to ever bring him up.

"Thanks for my stuff," I said calmly, knowing if I rose to the bait that it was his way of holding me hostage. Then, I turned on my heel and all but ran away from his house.

I slammed the box into the passenger seat of my car. I'd go through it when I got into work. I still had some time before my meeting. I was ninety percent sure that he'd purposely kept something else to lure me back to his doorstep. Certainly wouldn't put it past him.

I ripped the ticket off of my front window with an irritated growl and dropped into the front seat. Great. Just great.

This was just icing on the cake of a terrible day. I revved the engine and shot out onto the Savannah streets. At least I had a reserved parking spot for my business, and I pulled into it with relief. I pocketed the ticket, hefted the box into my arms again, and crossed Broughton Street to Ballentine—the fashion boutique that was my entire life.

I'd graduated from Parsons with a degree in fashion design, and after spending a couple of years in high-end clothing in Manhattan, I'd left that world behind to open my own business. A business that was currently *thriving*. Doing so well in fact that I had a meeting that afternoon about opening another location. I was excited and terrified, but anything was better than thinking about Mark.

The bell chimed softly overhead as I toed open the door to the store. My assistant was at the register, and half a dozen women were browsing the selections. Normally, I'd have a smile and kind word for every one of them, but I couldn't manage it. No amount of debutante and pageant work could force a smile out of me today.

"Rough day?" Sasha asked.

"Cancel everything I have this afternoon, except the Charleston meeting."

My assistant winced. "Mark?" she guessed.

"The devil," I growled.

Sasha shot me a sympathetic look, but I couldn't handle sympathy today. I wanted to hold on to my anger. That fire was necessary to survive. I had a pageant dress to finish, a business plan to hone, and a life-or-death meeting for the success of my boutique.

"There's one more thing," Sasha began.

"Save it for later."

I pushed past Sasha and into the back room. The door to my office was propped open. I frowned in confusion. Sasha was always careful about leaving it closed. If I had been robbed on top of the rest of today, I was going to fucking lose it.

But when I stepped into my office, there was already someone inside.

"Ash," I whispered.

The man of my dreams turned slowly to face me. He was dressed in a tailored navy-blue suit that hugged his broad shoulders and tapered sharply to his trim waist. The white button-up underneath was crisp and paired with a charcoal tie. His dark hair had been cut short on the sides with just enough length on the top to gel it into an artful appearance. And those perfect crystal-clear blue eyes were looking straight into me.

My heart fluttered at the sight of him. The uninterrupted sight. When I'd been dating Mark, I couldn't appreciate just how gorgeous he was. I wasn't supposed to notice that he was the most attractive person I had ever laid eyes on. And in this moment, it was almost impossible to remember that I was furious with him.

"Hey, Mia," he said with that heart-stopping smile.

"No," was the only word that came out of my mouth.

His smile dimmed. "No?"

"I cannot do this today." I dropped the box onto a chair and shook my arms out. "You should go."

"What's with the box?"

I glared at him. "I don't owe you answers."

"Mia..."

I closed my eyes against the pain of that nickname. Once upon a time, we'd been close enough that he could call me that. We'd been close enough that I thought we were finally going to get our happily ever after. But it wasn't like that for us. It never had been, and it never would be.

"I've had a really shitty day already, and I can't do whatever this is."

"You don't even know why I'm here."

I met his gaze. "You found out about me and Mark."

He shrugged. "I found out the day it happened."

"Really?" I asked with an arched eyebrow. "That was weeks ago."

"And I wanted to show up weeks ago."

"And yet..."

"I would have," he said quickly, "but Derek told me he'd kill me."

I snorted. "That sounds like my brother."

"He was right. He usually is."

Derek had been right. I'd needed the time to

decompress from the shit with Mark. It was hard enough, seeing Ash now. I would have blown a gasket if he'd shown up right afterward.

"Why are you here?" I demanded.

"Go to lunch with me."

Lunch. Ash and I had had a standing lunch date for years. Back when I'd been in love with him and he'd been my best friend. Back when things had been shockingly less complicated and so much sadder. Lunch was a death trap.

"No, thank you."

"Then, dinner," he pressed.

My heart flipped. Oh, how I would have died for him to ask me to dinner a year ago. I wished that it could have been enough. That any of it could have been enough.

I turned my back on that perfect smile and the little dimple that showed in his cheek. It was much harder to turn him down when I was looking at him. "I can't. I have a meeting."

"You have a meeting tonight?"

"I'm not going out with you, Ash."

His hand came to my arm, and he turned me to face him. "Amelia, I know that we handled this all wrong in the past. That was my fault. Please let me try to make this right."

I extracted my arm from his touch. The past had proven time and time again that this was never going to work the way I wanted it to. If I said yes today, then

K.A. LINDE

I'd never take that meeting. I'd never talk to a developer about opening another boutique in Charleston. I'd never leave my hometown and start over.

So, I shook my head. Ash Talmadge couldn't derail my plans. Not again.

"I can't," I choked out. "Please ... just go."

Ash looked like he wanted to say more. His hand hovered toward me as if he was going to try to change my mind. He could. I was certain of it. Ash had a persuasive flare that was unparalleled. He was a businessman. He got what he was after. I was the current pursuit, and I wanted to give in. I wanted it so badly that it ached. Yet I stood my ground.

He must have seen the resolution harden in my face. Because he finally nodded.

"Good luck with your meeting. Maybe another time." He straightened his suit and shot me one last searching look before stepping out of my office.

I sank into the chair behind my desk and buried my head in my hands. Today was a nightmare. And I couldn't shake the feeling that I'd fucked up horribly.

Ash Talmadge was the one person I'd always wanted. I'd wanted him for as long as I could remember. Seventeen-year-old me would have berated me endlessly for denying him a date. That innocent girl had wanted nothing more than for him to notice her. I remembered it like it was yesterday.

But I couldn't go backward.

Even if I wanted to.

2

SAVANNAH
DECEMBER 20, 2008

The text message made my eyes sting. I blinked fiercely a dozen times to keep the tears from collecting in my lashes. I'd been in hair and makeup all day. The debutante coordinator would kill me if I had tear tracks down my face. Even happy tears weren't allowed this close to my debut.

But the text was still there.

we have to break up i don't care bout this deb stuff sry

My now ex-boyfriend of six months, Brad, who had attended every debutante event with me since the start of the season, was acting like, *now*, he didn't care. This was the biggest night of my young life when I would be introduced to high society at the Christmas Cotillion. And now, I had no escort.

"Amelia," the coordinator, Mary called. "Amelia,

we're still waiting on Brad. He should have been here already."

I took a steadying breath and reached for my pageant smile. I'd won Miss Savannah only six weeks earlier. I was well on my way to Miss Georgia in the spring. Even if I hadn't had all the deb practice, I was skilled in holding back my emotions.

"I'm trying to find that out," I told her carefully.

Mary pursed her lips. "This will look unfavorably on you. Your escort should be prompt."

As if that were my fault.

"I understand. Let me figure out where he's at."

What I meant was, *Let me find a suitable replacement for my introduction and the inevitable waltz*, which Brad and I had been perfecting for several months. Dick.

I stepped away from the half-dozen other girls in similar white dresses and long white gloves and dialed my brother.

He answered on the second ring. "Mia?"

"I have an SOS situation."

Derek huffed on the phone. "What's going on?"

"Brad just ... dumped me."

"Fuck."

"He's not going to be here to escort me."

"What the fuck?" Derek demanded. "Do I need to find him and beat the shit out of him?"

I laughed softly. "Uh, no. Not enough time. I don't know what else to do. Will you walk me?"

My brother was four years older and a basketball

star at University of North Carolina-Chapel Hill. I was lucky enough that he'd been able to come home at all during Christmas break for my cotillion. He'd probably fly out to make a game tomorrow. But he'd escorted more than his fair share of St. Catherine's debs in his years as a Holy Cross boy. St. Catherine's was the all-girls Catholic high school and Holy Cross was the all-boys school next door. Thus, Derek knew the dance. It would be humiliating that I'd have to walk with my brother and not a date, but I was a Ballentine. My reputation could withstand the whispers.

"I've got you covered. Sending in reinforcements."

I laughed to hold back my tears. "Thanks, Derek."

Before Mary could ask where exactly my escort was again, I hustled out of the backstage area and to the locked side entrance. A knock came on the other side a few minutes later, and I pulled it open, expecting my brother.

Instead, I found Ash Talmadge.

I gaped at him, standing silhouetted in the doorway in a tuxedo. My heart literally stopped beating for a split second.

Ash was my brother's best friend. We'd grown up together since we were really little. Since his dad and my dad were also best friends. Even though he was two years younger than Derek, they'd had always hung out. We'd even vacationed together in the summer. But while the age difference didn't seem to matter for friends, Ash being two years older than *me*, twenty to my seventeen, *almost* eighteen, felt like an insurmountable difference. And yet I'd never wanted him more than in that moment.

"Hey, Mia," he said with a grin that revealed just the hint of a dimple.

"Ash," I gasped, quickly recovering. I threw my arms around him. "I had no idea you were coming to my debutante."

"Of course. I couldn't miss it."

"When did you get back from Duke?" I asked, gesturing for him to come inside.

"A couple days ago. When Derek invited me to your deb ball, how could I refuse? And I heard there was an incident with your boyfriend?"

I rolled my eyes. "Ex-boyfriend."

I showed him the text message. Ash's face was hot with anger.

"What a dick."

"Tell me about it." I hid my phone again in the pocket of my white deb dress. "So … I'm sort of without an escort."

"Ah, yes, well, I'm the reinforcements. I'll escort you if you'll have me."

My body practically listed toward him.

Good riddance, Brad. He was nothing compared to Ash. That was for damn sure.

"I would … love that," I said softly.

I wasn't sure if Ash knew what kind of effect he had

Wait for Always

on me. I wasn't exactly subtle in how I felt about him, but I'd basically been his kid sister for much of our lives. He and Derek would run off and make trouble while I tried to keep up with them and generally failed. I wanted there to be a moment when that all changed. When he saw me as more than just his best friend's little sister, but that only happened in movies.

"Amelia!" Mary called again.

"This way." I took Ash's hand in mine and pulled him down the hall.

Mary tapped her foot impatiently. A smile came to her mouth at the sight of my new escort. "Well, James, what a pleasure."

Ash grinned at Mary. "James is my father."

Ash was technically James Asheford Talmadge IV, but no one called him that. He was just Ash to us.

"Yes, yes." She waved her hand. "To what do we owe the pleasure?"

"He's my escort," I blurted out quickly.

The other debutantes gasped and tittered behind Mary. They were eyeing Ash with blatant jealousy. Their boyfriends or dates or escorts were all going to pale in comparison to him. A college boy this handsome was always a prized catch.

Mary arched an eyebrow. "Where's Brad?"

Ash cut in smoothly. "He's not good enough for our Amelia," Ash said affectionately. "Plus, we both know I can waltz better than anyone else here."

Mary softened. "That is true."

I was certain that Mary was going to get on me for Brad's absence, but a few words from Ash Talmadge, and she was putty in his hands too. Incredible.

Ash drew me in close as Mary put us in line. "There ... the night is salvaged."

"I think you just made her knees weak," I whispered.

He grinned and leaned in conspiratorially. "She actually has a thing for Derek."

I gagged. "Ew, Ash! She's, like, my mom's age."

He laughed. "Hey, older women can teach you things."

"Now, you're just trying to make me sick."

"I'm sure older guys can teach you things too."

"You're older than me," I shot back before the implication of my words hit me.

Ash's eyes traveled down to my lips and back up. My cheeks flushed. Time slowed to a crawl. Had Ash ever looked at me like that? Not as far as I knew. Only in my dreams. I wondered in that moment if, finally, all those dreams were about to come true.

Then, the moment burst like a popped bubble.

Ash straightened to his considerable height, as if realizing exactly who he was flirting with. "That's not what I meant."

I deflated slightly at those words. No, of course it wasn't what he'd meant. Ash Talmadge might have looked down at my lips, but as soon as he remembered

Wait for Always

that I was Derek's little sister and completely off-limits ... he'd never look at me like that again.

"Of course not," I said, forcing out my own laugh. "I was joking."

"Come on, deb." He offered me his arm. "Let's go show the world who their queen is."

Somehow, he still brought back my smile.

"There is no deb queen."

"There will be this year," he said confidently as he followed the line of debs toward the stage.

My stomach flipped at his words. Even if he wasn't thinking about me in a romantic sense, it didn't change a single thing about how I felt about him. It never had.

The rest of the presentation that I'd spent my life anticipating went by in a blur. I walked across the stage to raucous applause. A bouquet of roses was placed in my arms while I smiled my pageant smile. It was over in a matter of minutes. And suddenly, I was a lady in the eyes of society.

The traditional waltz was the last official step of the night. Ash took my hand and drew me onto the dance floor, and even though he hadn't waltzed in at least a year, we moved together as if we had been born to it. And we had been. A Ballentine and a Talmadge had been made for this.

"So, have you heard from colleges?" Ash asked as we passed another couple, who was struggling with the steps.

"Parsons." I beamed. "I just got my acceptance letter in the mail."

"Congratulations! And you're pursuing fashion design?"

"Yes. I'm so excited."

"I remember the outfits that you would make when we were younger. You wanted to put on a play for the Fourth of July, but we only had bathing suits and T-shirts. You stripped my mother's hundred-dollar curtains and made suitable outfits for the show. When my mother realized what you were wearing, she literally fainted."

I burst into laughter. "Oh my God, your mom never forgave me."

"She did," he assured me. "Your mom replaced them."

That part of the story I'd forgotten entirely. Mom and Dad had divorced when I was in middle school after he had an affair. He and Kathy had been married for years now, Mom had moved to Charleston to be near her brother, and I was the one stuck in the middle of it all. Sometimes, I forgot what it had been like when Mom was here and she and Dad didn't hate each other.

"That feels so long ago."

"I suppose it was," Ash agreed. "But the play was better with the new attire."

"It was, and, yes, I'll be doing fashion. I designed my deb outfit," I said, gesturing to my long white gown.

Wait for Always

"And I've been putting together a new gown for Miss Georgia."

"Which you will surely win," he said with a dashing smile.

I laughed. "Don't get ahead of yourself. It's a long jump from Miss Savannah to Miss Georgia."

The waltz came to a halt, and I let my arms drop. But Ash came forward, brushing a strand of loose dark hair off of my cheek. My heart thudded, and everything else seemed to disappear. The music dimmed. The rest of the debs were gone, and suddenly, we stood together, alone, on a crowded dance floor.

"You're going to win," he told me with utter confidence. "You don't know how to lose."

I wanted to step forward. I wanted to lean into him. Oh, how I had wanted that for so long. I would have given anything to have him see me in that moment. For it not to just be me craving this boy, but to have him desire me in return.

"Will you be there?" I asked, my voice breathy.

He smiled, and I was sure that I didn't imagine the hint of desire on his handsome face. "I wouldn't miss it for the world."

3

MISS GEORGIA
JUNE 27, 2009

"And the winner is ... Amelia Ballentine!"

My hands flew to my mouth as I gasped in shock. My runner-up pulled me in for a giant hug, congratulating me on my success. Then, the former Miss Georgia helped fit me into my crown, a bouquet of flowers was pushed into my arms, and I strode forward, smiling through my astonishment at my win.

Confetti rained down on the front seats. Tears threatened to run down my face. The crowd was on their feet for me. My entire world had come to watch me win this crown. They were currently seated to the left of the stage, and I waved. Their cheers rose even higher.

I'd been in pageants since I had been old enough to toddle on the stage. They were outdated, of course. As much as debutante balls. They were patriarchal bullshit. A way to get men and to have men ogle us and for women to be judged on their looks. But at the same time, it was *so* much more than that for me and all the other women on this stage. It was about doing good for the world, raising money for charity, and finding a platform to be heard as a woman. It was damn hard to have that in this world. If I had to strut in a bikini and a ball gown for a few judges so I could promote my platform, then so be it.

At the debutante ball earlier this year, I'd raised five thousand dollars to help get foster children clothing and supplies. Today, the entire state of Georgia had heard me discuss the need for a better foster system and the promise that, one day, I would open my own clothing boutique and donate proceeds to help.

All of this would be worth it in the end.

After the fanfare and pictures and interviews, I was finally released for the night and found my family waiting for me.

"Mom," I said, throwing myself into my mom, Margie's, arms.

After my obligations were over for the pageant, I would be going to Charleston to spend a few weeks with her, and I'd been looking forward to it all summer.

"You were incredible, sweetie."

"You really were," Kathy said, crowding in next to her.

My moms. Kathy was my stepmom, and I probably

should have hated her for breaking up my family. But she had been with my dad for five years and had been at every single event of mine. Even the ones that Mom couldn't drive in for because she was too busy with her interior design business.

I released my mom and threw my arms around Kathy. "Thank you for coming."

Kathy laughed and squeezed me tighter. "My little pageant queen. Of course, we all had to be here."

"Baby," my dad, Doug, said from behind my moms.

I released Kathy and stared at him. I'd always been a daddy's girl. I wasn't quite sure what I was now that he'd ruined everything. Sure, I'd gotten a second mom in the process, who I loved. He was still my daddy, but part of me hated him.

"I'm so proud of you," he said softly.

It was my mom urging me forward that got me to take the step in my heels. He wrapped his arms around me and kissed my forehead.

"You did amazing."

"Thanks, Daddy."

I broke away first and turned to find my brother.

Derek handed me another bouquet of flowers. "I knew you'd win."

I laughed. "Thanks, Derek."

My cousin Marina barreled into me, crushing my bouquets between our chests. "It was horribly outdated, but you were right, it was magic."

I snorted. Mom had driven Marina in from

Charleston. She was my closest friend. I'd never trusted any of the girls at school like I did Marina. We'd spent every summer together since we were kids, and I hated that this was going to be the last one.

"I can't believe you even came. You hate pageants."

"Yeah, well, I can't hate anything with you in it," Marina said matter-of-factly. She was the kind of dark-haired, blue-eyed girl next door that didn't have to try for everything that came her way. She was comfortable whether running for school president, wearing a homecoming queen crown, or fishing on one of her family boats.

"Thanks, Rina."

A throat cleared behind her, and my world shifted.

"Ash," I said in surprise. He'd told me at the deb ball that he'd be here, but that had been months ago. I hadn't been sure if he remembered … or cared.

He held out another bouquet of red roses. "Congratulations on your win."

I accepted them with a smile. "Thank you so much. I'm glad you came."

"I told you that I would."

Derek coughed. "My little sister."

Ash shot him a dirty look. "What? She did good."

Derek punched him in the arm. "I saw that look before."

My cheeks flushed at those words. I loved my older brother, but sometimes, he was so embarrassing. He could have let me and Ash have our moment.

"All right," my mom interjected. "It's late. Let's head back to the hotel. We can do brunch in the morning."

Everyone started talking at once, and I fell into step beside Marina. I glanced back once at Ash to find him looking right at me. Our eyes locked in the space between us. My stomach flipped as something solidified in that look. The same one I'd seen at the debutante ball when I considered being brave enough to kiss him. Then, Derek smacked him in the chest, breaking the look.

I turned back around to Marina, who arched a knowing eyebrow.

"We're talking about this later."

Marina had moved her stuff into my already-crowded hotel room when I was at the RiverCenter, getting ready for the pageant. I'd left most of my stuff in my backstage dressing room since I'd have all-day interviews and meet and greets tomorrow. But tonight, I was free.

Marina collapsed back on the king-size bed we'd be sharing. "So, are you going to *finally* put your tongue down his throat?"

I snorted. "Marina!"

"What? You have been into Ash Talmadge your entire life. And I saw that look he gave you."

"Yeah," I admitted. "It wasn't the first time."

She shrieked. "Excuse me? Why was I not informed?"

"You didn't come to my debutante ball."

Marina wrinkled her nose. "Those are so old-fashioned."

"You were homecoming queen!"

"Yeah, but, like, I gave my crown away to my friend Carol because they'd refused to let the lesbian couple be on the court, and I thought that was bullshit. She would have won if they hadn't been such bigots."

"That was the right thing to do," I admitted. "But still ... you let yourself be on the court. It's not that different."

She shrugged, conceding the point. "Fine. But back to the important thing: you've been keeping secrets. Tell, tell!"

"Well, I told you how he walked me at the ball because Brad dumped me."

"Yes."

"So ... there was a moment where he looked at my lips and then back up at me. And we were dancing, and there was this"—I sighed dramatically—"moment."

"Girl, you have it so bad. Can you just kiss him already?"

"When exactly would I do that? I'm going to Charleston with you when I leave here."

"Oh my God ... let's go out tonight!"

I blinked. "Where?"

"I don't know. The boys will know."

"The boys?"

Marina rolled her eyes. "Derek and Ash, obviously. What other boys? They'll know where to go out and get drunk."

"I *cannot* get drunk. I have interviews in the morning."

"Then, we'd better get started." Marina grabbed my hand and hauled me out of the room. She tiptoed past the rooms for my parents. She knocked on the door to the boys' room.

Derek answered, and my heart sank. Oh no.

"Hey, let's go out," Marina said mischievously.

"You're eighteen," he reminded her.

"And? As if I've never had a beer before. As if *you* never had a beer at eighteen," Marina countered. "I remember that one summer where Dare and I had to carry you back inside while Tye laughed his ass off."

Daron and Tye were Marina's brothers. Daron was two years older, and Tye was the same age as us, but he'd been adopted, so they weren't twins.

Derek held his hand up. "Don't remind me. I had a hangover for days."

"What's going on?" Ash asked, appearing at the door.

"They want to go out."

"Then, let's go out."

Derek shot him a look. "They're eighteen."

Wait for Always

"I'm twenty," Ash reminded him. "And anyway, what were you doing at eighteen, dipshit?"

"That's what I said!" Marina said.

"I'm not drinking," I said quickly because I knew Derek's real objection was for me and not Marina. He loved her too, but he was way overly protective of me. "I have interviews in the morning."

"Yes, you are!" Marina countered.

"Rina, shut up," I hissed.

"Come on, Derek," Ash said with a grin. "You wanted to meet up with that other girl anyway."

"What girl?" I asked at the same time Derek shrugged and said, "Fine."

Marina whooped, and I clapped a hand over her mouth. She giggled as we all looked down the hall. Only Derek was legally old enough to drink. The last thing we wanted was to alert the parentals.

Derek sighed heavily, pocketed his keys, and we all headed downstairs. Marina stood on her tiptoes and slung an arm over his shoulders, leaving me to stand beside Ash.

I glanced his way, and he smiled when he noticed me noticing him.

I flushed again. "Is this a bad idea?"

"Who cares? We're only young once," he said, holding the door open for me.

We followed Derek down the street. I prayed as I flashed a fake ID to the bouncer. I'd only ever used it at crappy places in Savannah. I'd never tested it elsewhere. Just what I needed was to get arrested the night after I won my title. I'd make the newspapers in the worst way. But the guy just smirked at my tits and then waved us all through.

"That was easier than I'd thought," Ash said.

Marina gestured to my V-cut pink dress. "That helps."

Ash's eyes dipped down and then quickly back up.

Derek just shoved Marina. "Keep moving."

Marina laughed, grabbed my hand, and tugged me toward the bar. She ordered Sex on the Beach for the both of us and immediately started flirting with a guy at the bar. Derek was speaking to another one of the pageant girls with skin the color of onyx, tightly coiled hair, and cheekbones so sharp that they could cut. I didn't remember her name, just that she was from the Atlanta area.

Ash stood next to him, looking bored by her friend, who was clearly trying to come on to him. I drank in his appearance. All tall, dark, and handsome with piercing blue eyes. He had on short-cut khaki shorts, a white button-up, rolled to his elbows, and boat shoes. The only boy I'd ever really wanted, and I was too scared to do a damn thing about it. I could conquer a stage in heels, but not tell the boy I liked that I liked him.

I turned my back on him and downed the drink quickly before ordering a second one. So much for not drinking, but, damn, I needed a little liquid courage. Marina was right. Tonight was the night.

I was on my third Sex on the Beach when the alcohol effects began to hit me. My legs were wobbly, and it was suddenly hot. I touched Marina's arm and told her I was going to get some air. Then, I pushed through the crowd and out onto the back tiki-decorated patio. June in Georgia was always sweltering with intense humidity, but at least the patio had the river breeze. I tugged my long hair off of my sticky neck and pulled it up into a high ponytail.

"You doing okay?"

I turned, leaning back against the railing, to find that Ash had followed me outside. "Yeah, I'm good."

"You were drinking those pretty fast." He gestured to the empty Sex on the Beach in my hand.

"Maybe too fast," I admitted.

"I thought you weren't drinking."

"What are you, my brother now?" I teased.

He moved to the railing next to me and leaned out toward the river. "I am definitely not."

My body warmed at the way he'd said that. I set my cup down on the railing and mirrored his position. Our arms brushed against each other. Fireworks burst in my stomach. Just a year earlier, I never would have imagined we'd be standing this close together. I'd felt like a little kid while he was off at college. Now, here we were.

I turned to appreciate the sharp outline of his jaw and that beautiful face. He smiled and faced me.

"What?" he asked.

"I'm glad you're here."

"Yeah?"

I nodded.

His eyes dipped down to my lips again. They lingered a space longer than they had at the ball before returning to my eyes. "Mia, you were amazing today."

"Yeah?"

"Yeah." He leaned forward, brushing a loose strand of my hair behind my ear. "I'm glad I was there to see it."

His hand was still on the side of my face, tilting my head up to meet his eyes. I listed toward him. My entire life, I'd had this desperate, unrequited love pulsing through me. I'd always known that I'd never have Ash Talmadge. Two years older and my brother's best friend. It would never happen. And right now, I was realizing that maybe I'd been wrong all along.

"Ash, I ... I want this," I whispered.

"This?" he asked as if he didn't know.

"You."

He should have pulled away. Remembered that Derek was his best friend. That he'd probably get punched for this if Derek ever found out.

Instead, he drew me closer.

"Fuck, Mia."

Wait for Always

And then I couldn't wait any longer. Screw gender norms. I had waited long enough for him.

I stood on my tiptoes and pushed my lips against his. He startled for a split second. A horrible second where I thought he'd pull away. But then he relaxed, drawing an arm around my middle and tugging me tight into him. A squeak left my lips as I was pressed firmly against his chest. His head angled slightly, and then he opened my mouth with the brush of his tongue.

Another gasp escaped me as I let him in. Time moved in slow motion as my heart skyrocketed, my stomach catapulted, and everything went fuzzy at the edges.

I was kissing Ash Talmadge.

I was *kissing* Ash Talmadge!

"Oh," I gasped as he pulled slightly back. Just far enough for our noses to brush. "Wow."

He laughed softly. "Wow?"

"You ... are a good kisser."

He laughed, pushing his hands up to cup my face, and kissed me again. Ash took control in that kiss and ruined me for all other kisses. Because there was no way that anything could compare to this here with him. I could live in an eternity of just this moment.

When he released me this time, my eyes fluttered open, and I stared up into his baby blues, entranced. But his face had fallen. He sighed and put more distance between us.

"We probably shouldn't be doing this."

"Why?"

"You're a little drunk." I opened my mouth to deny it, but he continued, "And Derek would kill me."

"So? I can handle Derek."

I'd wanted this for so long. So, so long. This couldn't be the end. I needed more. I needed everything. I wanted to beg for his love, but I knew that wouldn't work. I'd seen time and time again before my mom had left that begging for anyone to want you was a ticking time bomb. My dad had still left for Kathy. Our life had still imploded. I'd never stoop so low.

"It's just ... not the right time."

And I hated to admit how long I held on to those words. That we'd find our right time eventually. That something or someone wouldn't always be in our way. I was still waiting.

4

SAVANNAH
PRESENT

Sasha knocked once on my open office door. "Amelia?"

I looked up from the recent donation email I'd received from the Foster Foundation, a foster charity that my boutique worked with. I'd made promises all those years ago as Miss Georgia and meant all of them. The first thing I did when I started Ballentine was reach back out to the charity and figure out a donation schedule. I'd been active in the community ever since.

"Hey, Sasha, you should see this email," I said with a bright smile.

She walked around the desk and read over my shoulder. "Oh my God, Amelia! You're being recognized as Philanthropist of the Year for Foster Foundation, and they're going to hold a ball in your honor."

I laughed. "I can't believe it. I knew we'd been helping, but I didn't know it was *this* much."

"You're incredible."

"I'll have to design a new dress."

"Hell yes!"

I was still beaming when I remembered Sasha must have been here for a reason. "Was there a problem? How is the new cashier?"

Sasha handled a lot of the day-to-day stuff for Ballentine. She was the best manager that I'd ever had. She was definitely in need of a promotion and raise. Especially if everything worked out with a new boutique in Charleston.

"New cashier is great. She already had retail experience. But that's not why I'm here."

My stomach sank. Oh. Oh, I knew what was coming. "He's here again?"

Sasha nodded. "Like clockwork."

Every day for the last ten days, Ash had shown up at the boutique. Most days, he asked me to lunch and then left when I turned him down. Wednesday, he'd left lemon bars from Back in the Day Bakery. The next Monday, he'd brought me a giant sweet tea from a local coffee shop. I was half-worried that he'd keep bringing me all of my favorite things until I said yes to lunch. Not that I planned to after the shit that had gone down last year.

"Will you tell him that I'm not free for lunch?"

Sasha shot me a look. "You *are* free for lunch."

"Yeah, but he doesn't need to know that."

"Or you could just talk to him."

Wait for Always

I sighed. "I *have* talked to him, and since when are you giving relationship advice?"

"Since my boss isn't seeing sense."

I couldn't help it. I laughed. "Is that so?"

Sasha sank into her hip and flipped her rainbow hair over her shoulder. "For one, have you seen that man? He is gorgeous. Two, he has shown up every single day to ask you out. That's so romantic."

"Or creepy."

She rolled her eyes. "It'd be creepy if you didn't know him and he wasn't a friend and you weren't totally into him."

"I'm not," I lied.

"You're not a good liar, Amelia. Everyone with eyes can see you're into him. You used to go to lunch with him for years. Even when he was with someone else. Now that you're both single, you're not going to give him the time of day? What did he *do* to you?"

It wasn't so much what he'd done as what he hadn't done. Years of what he hadn't done. Until it had all hit a fever pitch a year earlier. I didn't know how to come back from it. I'd loved him for so long, and I'd finally given up. How much more could I handle?

When I didn't respond, Sasha sighed. "Fine. But at least talk to him. I'm not telling him no again."

Then, she strode out.

Well, she was right. I didn't pay her to deal with my relationship issues. This was on me. I'd have to respond to the email from Foster Foundation afterward.

Despite myself, I pulled up the camera on my phone and checked my makeup, reapplying a bit of red lipstick and flattening my dark hair. I spritzed some Chanel No. 5 on my wrists and neck, internally yelled at myself for caring at all, and then forced myself to walk out of my office.

Ash was at the cash register, charming Sasha with a smile. He was in a charcoal suit today with a pink button-up and navy tie. That pink shirt was probably my favorite, and he knew it. Damn.

As soon as I came out of the back, his eyes shot over to me. They crawled down my figure and then back to my eyes. He straightened with a smile. "Hey."

I swallowed. "Hi."

The boutique was busy, as it was every lunch break. The last thing I wanted was a crowd of gossipmongers listening in on this conversation. I gestured for Ash to follow me out onto Broughton Street.

"You look lovely," he told me once outside.

"Thank you. Why are you here?"

"I wanted to see if you wanted to get lunch."

I blew out a harsh breath and ran a hand back through my hair. "Are you going to keep coming back every day?"

"Yes."

"You realize it's harassment. My dad and brother are lawyers."

Wait for Always

Ash shot me a smile. "I'm aware of their professions, yes. They work for me regularly." Then, his smile faltered. "If you really feel like I'm harassing you, then I'll stop. I just miss you, Mia."

I closed my eyes against those words. "Ash ..."

"I've missed you every day since we fought and I fucked up. Please," he said softly. "Just ... please."

Something cracked in me at that word. And when I found those baby blues again, I knew that I was a goner. That this was all I'd wanted for so long. And though I'd said I was done waiting, here I was, giving in all over again.

"One more chance," I finally said.

His smile immediately blossomed, revealing his dimples. "Lunch?"

"I'm serious, Ash."

"I'm taking you seriously, Mia."

"Then, yes. Let's go to lunch."

"You won't regret this."

I shook my head with a small laugh. "I'd better not. Let me grab my stuff."

I hurried back inside, throwing my phone into my purse. Sasha sent me a bright smile and a thumbs-up. I rolled my eyes, but I couldn't keep the smile from my lips. God, why did Ash always do this to me?

Ash had somehow managed to snag the parking spot directly in front of my shop. He'd upgraded recently to a black Range Rover and pulled the passenger door open for me like the Southern gentleman he was. I slid in across the black leather and buckled up. He jogged around to the driver's side, and after he was seated, he pulled away from the boutique.

"Clary's?" he asked.

I nodded. "Of course."

Clary's was my favorite restaurant in all of Savannah. They did all-day breakfast and had to-die-for biscuits and gravy. The biscuits were so fluffy, as if you were biting into a cloud, and the white gravy had sausage and was heavily peppered, as it should be.

Despite the crowd, we were seated immediately.

"You had a reservation?" I asked in surprise.

He shot me a look once we took our seats. "Well, I might have had one on the books for every day ... just in case."

My heart was made of candle wax, and he applied the flame. Everything melted at his heat.

"Oh," I whispered, hoping I held back my emotions well enough, but I never knew with Ash. He knew me too well.

We ordered food and made small talk while we waited for it to arrive. For those few minutes, everything felt normal. Like how it used to be when I'd first returned from New York City and Ash and I met up all the time.

"So," he began slowly after our regular topics dried up, "what happened with Mark?"

I winced and shoved my food away. "We broke up."

"You broke up with him."

"I did." I sighed and reached for my sweet tea. "What do you want to know? Mark was a narcissistic jerk who gaslit me. He told me that no one else wanted me and treated me like crap. I don't know why it took me so long to see what he was doing. But I finally broke free."

Ash's grip on his knife was murderous. "Jesus Christ, Amelia."

"Yeah."

"Are you all right? Do I need to go beat the shit out of him?"

I snorted. "No. You do not need to do that. You're not my white knight. The princess saved herself in this one."

He smiled. "I like that."

"Plus, if he saw you, he'd probably lose his shit."

"Saw that firsthand."

"Right," I muttered.

"Which I'm sorry about," he said.

I waved my hand. "It's over with. I don't care what he thinks anymore."

"Then, why wouldn't you see me?" he said, reaching across the table for my hand. "I know I fucked up, and that pushed you into his arms."

I slowly extracted my hand from his. "Don't flatter yourself. I made my own bad choices."

"Well, if I hadn't acted that way—"

"Please," I said, holding up a hand, "let's not rehash the past."

The night had been bad enough. I thought about it for weeks afterward. I'd thought about it all those times that I realized that Mark was not a better alternative. I was tired of thinking about it. Tired of agonizing over if me and Ash could have had a better outcome.

"All right," he said softly. "Well, I've missed you. I'm glad you're single."

I laughed softly. "Me too. I feel free for the first time in a long time."

I waited for him to ask me out again, as he had last week when he showed up at the boutique. To push for more after I agreed to lunch. I'd been anticipating it. Trying to figure out how to say no to him again, only to realize that I wouldn't. If he asked me out again, I'd say yes.

I didn't know if that made me weak. If it did, then Ash Talmadge made me weak. I wasn't going to settle for less from him this time. I'd meant it when I said it was our last chance.

But Ash didn't ask me out. He just grabbed the bill and paid before I could reach for it. A knowing smirk on his too-pretty lips.

Then, he held his hand out and asked, "Leopold's?"

A man after my heart. Ice cream was always the answer.

5

SAVANNAH
PRESENT

"I'll take two scoops of the chocolate chip, and she'll have scoops of butter pecan and pistachio, both in a cone," Ash ordered for the both of us before I could even open my mouth.

"Coming right up."

"I can order for myself," I told him.

He smirked. "But you always get the same thing. You have since we were kids."

"Not true. I went through a strawberry phase."

"That was one summer," he reminded me. "And I think it was just to prove Derek wrong."

I rolled my eyes at him. It had actually been to prove Derek wrong. "Whatever."

We took our cones, and Ash went to pay.

I tried to scoot around him. "You got lunch!"

He didn't budge and tapped his credit card. "So?"

"I can pay for things too."

"You are capable of that, yes, but not when you're with me."

"Just because you're a Talmadge and have more money than God doesn't mean that I can't buy us ice cream."

He pocketed his wallet and gave me the same smile that had made my knees weak since I'd been fifteen. "Yes, it does."

There was no point in arguing. I'd never paid for a thing around him. My family had nearly as much money as the Talmadges, and my boutique was doing wonderful, but there was no way I made close to what he did. Not yet at least.

"You're an ass," I muttered under my breath as I took the first lick of my cone.

Ash laughed softly. He'd clearly heard me. "Who knew chivalry was dead?"

I rolled my eyes at him, and suddenly, everything felt totally normal again. "I'd say, most people, considering it was a knight's code of conduct in medieval times. All about honor and justice, are you?"

"Modern terms of chivalry," he corrected.

"Like stepping in at my debutante ball?"

Ash's eyes softened at the edges. "Indeed."

I knew what he'd meant, but it was fun to mess with him. In fact, as we took our seats under the Spanish moss in Reynolds Square, I realized just how much I'd missed Ash. Things had gotten turned upside down, but underneath it all was the friendship I'd had with him my whole life. Even when I'd been too young and he'd only seen me as an annoying little sister. Even when things had changed between us that time at Miss Georgia. Even much later ... when we'd said things we couldn't take back. I wished there were a way that we could hold on to this part of our relationship without reminding me of everything else. But I didn't know if that was possible.

"So, how did your meeting go?" Ash asked after I was quiet for too long.

"Oh," I muttered.

And then there was that. The part that he didn't know.

"It went well."

"What was it about anyway?"

I bit my lip and then decided to just get it over with. It wasn't like us getting lunch or ice cream was going to derail my plans.

"I'm looking at opening another boutique."

His eyes shifted to mine. Blue meeting blue. The world skittered to a halt in that one look. Confusion in them, followed by pride. "That's incredible. Who did you meet with?"

The question was so innocuous. Or it would have been if Ash hadn't been the person to help me get the property for my store on Broughton. He'd been with me the entire time. If I wanted to open another location in Savannah, I would go to him.

I swallowed and met his gaze again. "Holden Holdings."

Ash froze in place. "In Charleston?"

"Yes."

He opened his mouth and closed it. Of course he knew who Holden Holdings was. It was one of the most prominent companies on the southeastern coast, and he'd gone to college with the CEO, Nolan Holden. Ash had introduced us.

Finally, he asked, "Are you ... planning to run it from here?"

"No," I whispered.

A flash of panic shot across his features.

I continued speaking before I could stop myself. "I was planning to move to Charleston. Marina said I could stay with her while I got situated. Mom offered too, but I loved the idea of living with Marina."

"You could open another store here," he said. "There's plenty of space."

"I've thought about it, but I don't think the clientele is there." When he didn't say anything, I rushed forward. "Eventually, I'd like to open a store all up and down the coast—Hilton Head, Wilmington, Myrtle Beach, Jacksonville. And maybe if that did well, I could start doing college towns—Athens, Columbia, Chapel Hill."

"Which you could run out of Savannah," he said reasonably.

"Maybe."

Wait for Always

There was so much more to say. So much that I didn't know how to explain to him. I loved having Kathy close, but I hardly ever talked to my dad anymore. Derek had moved to Atlanta to be with his wife, Marley. Everyone else I loved was in Charleston. The only person who had kept me here was currently sitting beside me, staring back at me in disbelief. He'd been my lifeline in Savannah. And as much as it was home, it was haunted. One of the most haunted cities in the US, and full of ghosts of my life.

"I'm going in a few weeks to see my family and to meet with a Holden representative," I explained.

"Go out with me."

I sputtered, my eyes going wide. "What?"

Ash reached forward, sliding his hand into mine. "Go out with me, Amelia."

"No," I whispered breathily.

"Why not?"

"I've waited so long for you." I glanced down at our locked hands. The feeling so natural, so normal. And yet ... he had never been mine. "I've waited my whole life for you. You can't do this just because I might be leaving."

"I'm not," he said at once.

I arched an eyebrow. "Your response to me telling you about Charleston was to ask me out. How can I think otherwise?"

"You might remember that I came by the store last week and asked you out then too. That I've been coming by to see you every day. That I'm here right now. I want you to go out with me. I want this."

I closed my eyes around those words. Ones I would have literally died to hear when I was younger. When he'd loved someone else ... and I'd just been a consolation prize.

"Why?" I whispered.

"What do you mean?"

I stood up, pulling my hand free. It was one of the hardest things I'd ever done. "Why? Why do you want to go out with me? Why now? Why after everything?"

Why not before? That was what I wanted to ask, but he must have seen it on my face because whatever anger he'd been rising to meet disappeared.

"Because living without you was torture."

My heart stopped. "What?"

"It was torture. I hated every day and every minute without you. I've never experienced anything like it."

I scoffed. "I was there when Lila left you at the altar. I remember you drowning yourself in alcohol to try to forget. I remember all the stupid shit you did to try to move past what had happened with her. You want me to believe it was worse than that?"

But Ash didn't flinch away from what I'd said. The love of his life had left him on their wedding day for another man. We never spoke about it. We never said her name. And the time that I had slipped up was ... a catastrophe. Except this time, he really seemed different. I didn't know if he'd ever get over Lila entirely. I'd never been sure if that would actually happen, not when he'd wanted her as long as I'd wanted him, but for the first time, I saw something else in his eyes. Hope.

"No," he said finally. "It wasn't worse than that, but it was a different sort of terrible."

At least he was honest. I wouldn't have believed him if he'd said it was worse than the day of his wedding. But I could believe that he'd been hurting. I could see it on his face.

"It was," I admitted.

A smile cracked through his features and then disappeared again. He almost looked ... uncertain. But I'd never seen Ash look anything but confident.

"Look, what Lila and I had was ... toxic. I know that now. We were on and off for years, and now, she's marrying someone else. We had our chance. We had our chance too many times." He stepped forward, that confidence returning as he brushed a strand of my hair out of my face. "But you and I, we never had our chance. And I would regret it for the rest of my life if we didn't try, Mia."

A cool breeze cascaded between us as soft light filtered down through the hundred-year-old trees. The thousands of azaleas that overtook Savannah in the spring were just beginning to bloom. And all of it disappeared at Ash's words. The words I'd wanted for too long.

I was leaving for Charleston. I had plans to open

another boutique. I'd made these plans while plotting to get out of my relationship with Mark. Never thinking that I'd finally get my shot with Ash. Never thinking that he'd finally be over Lila. But here he was, talking about her in the past tense, admitting that they had been toxic and she was marrying someone else. I'd walked away for so much less, and I'd always wanted so much more. How could I say no when he was saying everything I'd wanted to hear?

"Okay," I finally said.

"Okay?"

I nodded. "I'll go out with you."

6

PARSONS
MAY 23, 2013

"You made it," I said with a smile.

Ash passed me a bouquet of red roses. "Like I'd miss it. Happy graduation."

My heart was in my throat as I took the roses. I knew they didn't mean anything. That he was dating Lila again. They'd dated briefly in high school and reunited after college. Derek had told me once how annoying they were but that he was glad Ash was happy.

And so I swallowed back that same desire that always rose up when I saw him. He was happy with someone else. I was currently dating someone too. I'd come a long way since that eighteen-year-old girl, drunk enough to steal a first kiss with him.

"I'm glad you're here," I told him.

"Yeah, yeah," Derek said, throwing an arm across

Ash's shoulders and leaning forward. "We're all thrilled."

Ash shoved him off. "Shut up. We know you begged me to come up for it."

Derek grinned. "Yeah. Well, it was more so I could get you to spend the week in Cambridge with me before graduation. You don't have time for me anymore now that you're a settled man."

"Fuck off, dude," he said with a laugh.

"It's just like old times," I said.

Ash had always been there at family events when I was younger. Our summer vacations in Charleston, my dad's second wedding, my sweet sixteen—he was always present. His parents sometimes joined him, but since he was an only child, half the time, they just sent him off with us. My parents had never minded, and Derek had liked having another boy to hang out with. Having him here felt right. And I couldn't deny that I was glad he hadn't brought Lila. We'd cheered together her senior year at St. Catherine's, but I didn't really know her. And since she had Ash's heart, I had no interest in getting to know her either.

"Yeah, just like me and Ash out on the sailboat in Charleston and you begging to be included," Derek joked.

I narrowed my eyes. "It's my college graduation. Must you be a dick?"

He ruffled my hair. "It's how I show love."

"I'm sure Marley loves it."

Ash and Derek exchanged a look. Boy code that I'd never been able to decipher. You'd think that they'd be spending all their time together since Lila and Marley were best friends and Ash and Derek were too. But it seemed like something was up with that, and I could never figure them out.

"Aren't you dating someone now?" Derek interjected. "Where is he anyway?"

My cheeks flushed. Camden Percy wasn't exactly the kind of guy who came to graduations. I wasn't sure what to make of him, except that he was, like, the richest guy on the planet, and somehow, he was interested in me. Sometimes, being in his presence felt like clinging on to the side of a boat for dear life. Like he was a force of nature that could never be weathered, you just prayed that it didn't destroy your entire world. I'd never met anyone else like him. Maybe that was what I liked about him.

"We're meeting up with him tonight," I said quickly.

I hadn't told Derek that I was dating Camden, who he knew from Harvard. He'd introduced us over spring break, but I was sure Derek hadn't done it so that we'd end up together.

Ash frowned. "Who is this mystery guy?"

Did I detect a note of jealousy?

No, that was absurd. Ash was with Lila. She was all he'd ever wanted, right? I nearly gagged on the thought.

"You'll just have to wait and see."

Kathy pushed between the boys and pulled me in for a hug. "We're so happy for you, sweetie."

"Thanks, Kathy."

Mom stood off to the side with her new boyfriend. She'd been with Jared for two years, but I never got the impression that she cared whether or not they got married. Maybe she didn't want to be tied down after what had happened with Dad.

"My baby is all grown up," she said with tears in her eyes.

"Mom," I said with a laugh, turning from Kathy to hug her. "I'll always be your baby."

"Yes, but now, you're going to be working for a high-end fashion designer on the Upper East Side. Your dreams are coming true."

I beamed. My dreams *were* coming true. I hadn't told anyone that Camden had helped me get the interview with a fashion designer. Elizabeth Cunningham was *the* designer on the Upper East Side. She had killed it at Fashion Week, and her sales were through the roof. Anyone who was anybody wanted to be wearing her. Even Katherine Van Pelt was wearing her clothes. It was sort of weird to think that I knew the ice princess of the Upper East Side, but she ran in the same circles as Camden, and we'd met once or twice. Camden looked at her like she was poison infecting everyone around her, but I wasn't sure why everyone hated her. People just didn't like when women succeeded, and she was currently on every runway and in every tabloid and the face for half of my favorite brands.

And now, *I* would be working with Elizabeth Cunningham. I was still dizzy with the knowledge that I'd start next week. I'd only met with Harmony Cunningham, her daughter, who also modeled for the label. But I was hoping I'd get to meet Elizabeth soon too.

Dad had his hands in the pockets of his suit when he smiled at me. "I always knew you'd do it."

"Thanks, Daddy," I said and let him hug me too.

And in that moment, I forgot all the other bullshit. My family was here. My life was moving in the right direction. That was all that mattered.

"Wait," Derek said as we took the elevator up Percy Tower to Club 360.

"Yes?" I asked. I checked the delicate Rolex on my wrist, which had been a birthday gift from Camden.

"Where are we going?"

"Club 360. I already told you."

He snatched up my wrist. "Where did you get this?"

I yanked my hand away. "It was a gift from my boyfriend."

Derek's eyes narrowed. "Who is this guy, Amelia?"

"Look, I don't need the *protective older brother* routine right now."

"If you think you're going to get it, then you probably already know that whatever this is, it's a bad idea."

I looked to Ash for backup, but he had his arms crossed, letting us duke it out.

"Whatever, Derek. You introduced us."

"Fucking hell," Derek said, leaning back against the elevator. "You're dating *Camden*?"

"So what if I am?"

"Fucking hell," he grumbled.

"He's *your* friend."

"Which is how I know that you shouldn't be dating him!" Derek snapped. "The guy owns this hotel. He owns the penthouse on top of the hotel. He owns the club that we're about to walk into. He owns everything in his life. I don't want him to own you too."

"He doesn't *own* me," I said with an eye roll.

Derek grabbed my wrist again and held up the diamond-encrusted watch. "What's this then?"

"A watch," I snarled.

His eyes widened. "And the new job?"

"I got that job on my own!"

"And he didn't put in a word? He owns the Upper East Side, Amelia. I know this guy."

"So?"

"This is a bad idea," Derek said grumpily. He nudged Ash. "Tell her, Ash."

Ash finally looked up at me. Our eyes met in that

Wait for Always

short distance. He hadn't said much this weekend. There was always something keeping him from his usual buoyant self.

He just shrugged. "Let me meet the guy first."

"Oh, great. So now, you're both going to be judging him."

"If I didn't think he'd put a hit on me, I'd beat the shit out of him for touching you," Derek said.

"Put a hit on you," I said with a head shake. "You're so dramatic. He's not in the Mafia!"

The elevator door dinged open, and we were on the top floor of Percy Tower, a highlight of the Upper East Side glam. I pushed away from my brother and to the front door. At the entrance, a line had of desperate men and women hoping to get into the club tonight had already formed.

"Hi, Jerry," I said with a smile at the bouncer.

"Amelia," he said with a nod as he pulled back the rope to let me through.

"They're with me."

Derek and Ash followed behind me to the grumbles of those in line. I knew exactly where Camden would be waiting for me. He always had a reserved booth, and just as I expected, he was standing around, drinking with his friends, Court and Gavin. A girl I recognized was seated at his side, laughing at everything he said. Her name was on the tip of my tongue ... *Fiona?*

Camden's eyes found me before I got to the table. A

shiver ran down my spine at the possessiveness in that one look. Maybe Derek wasn't wrong. Maybe he did own me. Because in that moment, I would have done anything for him.

He wasn't as tall as Derek and Ash, but he was still much taller than me with dark hair and dark eyes, wearing a two-thousand-dollar tailored suit. He extracted himself from his friends, slid an arm around me, and kissed me hard on the mouth.

"Hey, baby," I said breathlessly.

"How was graduation?"

"Perfect."

"Good." He nodded his head.

He didn't say he wished that he could have been there. He'd never say something that he didn't believe, and I thought he was glad I wasn't a college student anymore. He was in his late twenties, and I always felt a little out of place with his older friends. It was better when it was just the two of us.

"You remember Derek?" I said with a smile.

Derek stuck his hand out, and they shook. "Fucker," Derek muttered.

Camden grinned like the devil he was. "You should have known better when you brought her this spring."

"I should have," Derek said. "Don't make me punch you."

"Now, that would be entertaining. Punching the owner of the building you're standing in probably wouldn't go well for you."

Wait for Always

"Derek, Jesus," I groaned.

"And you are?" Camden asked Ash as he came to stand at Derek's side.

"This is Ash Talmadge."

Camden considered him for a moment. "Are you related to James Talmadge?"

"That's my father," Ash told him.

They didn't shake hands. Ash hadn't even offered, which was so unlike him.

"Ah, that makes sense. We've considered putting in a Percy Tower on River Street. I was working with your father on that, but it never panned out."

"You can't put a Tower on River Street," I argued immediately.

Camden looked down at me, as if he'd forgotten I had opinions. "And why not?"

"Because you'd ruin the view," Ash said as if it were obvious.

"And the history," I added. "Big hotels go across the river."

"Or on Bay Street," Ash finished for me.

Derek shrugged. "Locals know that sort of thing."

"I'm not used to people telling me no," Camden said with a smile that could have meant anything.

Derek clapped him on the back. "It happens to us measly mortals."

Camden arched an eyebrow at Derek, but whatever animosity had been between them at me dating Camden was gone. Camden gestured for us to come back to the booth. We followed Camden, and I met Fiona again. I'd been right about her name.

She kept giving me weird looks that I didn't understand. Maybe she was jealous. Derek invited her out to dance at some point, and I followed with Camden, leaving Ash alone with the guys.

We were on the dance floor when Katherine Van Pelt showed up in a blood-red dress that made her tall model body look like she was literally wearing the liquid. Her dark hair was a cascade down her back, and she laughed with her friends. All people I recognized—Penn Kensington, Lark St. Vincent, Archibald Rowe, and Lewis Warren. They were maybe the most beautiful people I'd ever seen. As if being on the outside, looking in, was as close as anyone could get to their crew.

Camden grumbled something low under his breath. "I have to handle something."

"I ..."

But he was already gone. Leaving me alone on the dance floor without another word.

I turned in a circle before pushing my way back toward the booth. It was empty, and I took a shot of tequila to steady myself. I didn't know what to think about Camden. I felt like I could chase him forever and never quite know him. Sometimes, it was as if I were on the outsider. Like I couldn't figure out what someone like him saw in someone like me. And then I hated myself for feeling that way.

But when he disappeared like that without considering how I'd feel, it made it hard not to be frustrated.

I should have just stayed and danced with everyone else, but I didn't have it in me. That was when I saw Ash Talmadge leaning against the edge of the rooftop bar, drinking whiskey.

I snagged another beer and headed toward him. "Hey."

His eyes found mine and looked away. "Hey."

"You've been quiet."

He shrugged. "Have I?"

"Yeah. Do you want to dance?"

It was a bad idea. Camden wasn't the sort of guy to handle me dancing with someone else. Not that he knew anything about Ash ... or how I'd felt about him my whole life.

"I'm not in the mood," he said, taking another sip of his drink.

"Okay," I said.

I waited for him to say something else, but he didn't. He brooded there, looking out across at the city below.

I couldn't do this tonight. It was my graduation, and I had a boyfriend. I didn't want to think about Ash Talmadge at all.

"Suit yourself," I finally said and then went back in search of Camden.

But when I found him, my stomach flipped. He was in the back room with his buddies and Fiona. She had a little bottle filled with white powder, and they were passing it around. Plenty of people in my program had done cocaine. Enough of them that it became this design party where they'd all get high and try to make their outfit for the week in one night. I'd never joined in any of those parties.

And it wasn't like I was upset with Camden for doing it here. I just ... hadn't known. Suddenly, I felt really young again. Twenty-two and utterly clueless in these matters.

I backed out of the room before any of them could see me. My heart wouldn't calm down, and I felt unbalanced. Like a kid seeing their parents doing something wrong.

I returned to the balcony edge, downing the rest of my beer in one long gulp. Then, Ash was again next to me.

"What's wrong?" he asked.

I blinked at him in surprise. "What?"

"You seem upset."

"It's nothing. Why are you being so weird tonight?"

"I'm not being weird," he said. "I just ... don't think you should be dating him."

I snorted. "Okay, *Derek*."

He huffed. "I said I wanted to meet him before forming an opinion."

"And he's not good enough for me?"

"No. He's not," he said flatly.

"He's Camden Percy," I argued.

"That doesn't mean anything."

"It does here."

"Then, maybe you should get out of New York."

I narrowed my eyes at him. I was getting upset again. "My *life* is in New York. I have this amazing new job and a boyfriend and friends."

"Savannah is home."

"So?" I spat back at him, pushing off of the edge to glare at him. "Ash, why do you even care? You're not my brother. And you're certainly not *single*. You don't get to have an opinion about all of this."

"I know that kind of guy, Mia," he said, grabbing my arm before I could walk away. "I've seen plenty of guys like him treat girls like you like shit. I can recognize it when I see it. He's an asshole."

"Can you recognize that you're being an asshole?" I jerked my arm back. "Let me go."

He dropped my arm. "Amelia ..."

"What are you, jealous?"

He stood there in surprise. As if he had never considered the option before. And that hurt all the more.

"Just ... go home to Lila, Ash."

Then, I turned and walked away from him. A part of me knew that he was right, but I just wasn't ready to admit it. But at the same time ... he wasn't ready to admit his jealousy either. So, I didn't owe him anything.

7

NEW YORK CITY
OCTOBER 17, 2014

"I'm out early today, Shannon," I reminded my manager.

Her eyes were wide. "What? Who approved that?"

I paused, fear spiking through me. It always did that at Elizabeth Cunningham. It didn't matter if I'd gotten the time off approval ages ago. Working in high fashion was as terrifying as *The Devil Wears Prada* made it out to be and sometimes worse. The adrenaline hit when I had to eat lunch and it was something other than a salad or getting coffee and it wasn't skinny. The pressure was intense. Taking time off was worse.

"You ... you did," I reminded her. I pulled up our shared app and showed it to her. "See, I have a half-day today and Monday off."

"How are you going to make up this time?" Shannon asked.

Wait for Always

"I can stay late the rest of the week. My brother and his best friend are in town for the weekend."

"I didn't approve this." Shannon looked like she was going to have a panic attack.

That was when Harmony Cunningham slipped in. "Actually, I did."

I blinked in surprise. Harmony mostly modeled for the company, but her mom had slowly been giving her more responsibilities. All things considered, I liked Harmony way more than everyone else. Her mom was a nightmare.

"Oh, thank you, Harmony."

"No problem, Amelia. And don't worry about making up the hours. I'll be in for the rest of the day and Monday to help around."

Shannon opened her mouth to object, but Harmony shot her an imperious look, and Shannon dropped it. I'd realized that about Harmony. Few people could argue with her and win. The only person I'd seen her have a full-blown argument with was Katherine Van Pelt. It had been a thing of nightmares during Fashion Week. All over a guy at that. I mean, Penn Kensington was gorgeous, but he wasn't worth your career. Not that either of them was likely to lose it with the connections they had, but still!

"Go have fun, and if you want to bring the boys, we'll be at 360 tonight!" Harmony offered.

I flinched and hated that I still did. Club 360 belonged to Camden, and I no longer did. I didn't go there anymore unless I was dragged with fashion friends since it was the place to see and be seen.

"I'll pass, but thanks for the offer."

Harmony followed me toward the entrance. "Hey, don't let Camden keep you away. Fuck that guy."

I laughed. "Thanks, Harm. It's not him. I just want to spend time with my family, you know?"

Harmony gave me a sympathetic look, like she didn't believe me. And hey, I didn't believe me either.

"Next time," she offered like an olive branch.

"Definitely. Bye."

"Have fun!"

I waved good-bye as I stepped out onto Madison Avenue in my all-black outfit and black high heels, wrapping my black peacoat around my shoulders. What I wouldn't give for some color in my wardrobe, but that just wasn't *done*. In Savannah, I'd grown up in pastels, but I couldn't imagine anyone in New York fashion wearing lavender or mint. This was what I'd signed up for.

I was nearly to my apartment in the West Village when I got a text from Derek, saying that they were almost there. Derek had moved back to Savannah to take his place in our family law firm in August after he'd finished up a year of working for one of his Harvard professors. Though I knew the real reason was the big breakup with Marley.

Which was why Ash was here with him. Something had gone down with him and Lila. Bad enough that Derek had gotten him out of Georgia as soon as possible, and he was about to be in my apartment for four days. I didn't know the details, just that they'd broken up after almost two years together and he was a wreck.

Maybe I shouldn't have been excited … but I was.

I came out of the subway at Washington Square Park and just closed the door behind me at my Cornelia Street apartment when the buzzer rang.

I pressed the button. "Come on up."

After a cursory look at my apartment, I grabbed a stray bra off the back of a chair, which I had somehow missed in my sweep last night, and decided it was good enough. If it had just been Derek, I wouldn't have even cleaned up. He didn't give a shit. He was my brother. But Ash …

Well, I cared too much about Ash.

A knock at the door drew me away from my frantic cleaning. I yanked it open and found Ash leaning against the doorframe while Derek carried both suitcases up the stairs.

"Hey," he said with a smirk. He was in a white button-up, rolled up to his elbows, and black dress pants. His suit coat was slung over his shoulder.

"Hi," I said.

"He's already drunk," Derek grumbled. "Asshole couldn't even carry his own bag."

"I'm not drunk," Ash said, running a hand back through his dark hair.

"It was a good thing we flew first class," Derek said. He shoved past Ash into my apartment. "Or else you would have paid your weight in alcohol on that flight."

I arched an eyebrow at Ash. "That bad?"

Ash shrugged as he shuffled inside. "I'm fine."

Derek snorted. He dropped the bags inside the small apartment. "Fine. Sure."

I doubted very much that he was fine. He didn't look fine. And if he was drunk already, that wasn't a good sign either. What the hell had happened with Lila?

"Let's go get a drink," Ash said.

"I have some beer in the fridge. Help yourself," I told him. "I have to change out of work clothes."

Ash's eyes swept down my chic outfit. He arched an eyebrow. "You look better in color."

I froze at those words. They perfectly mirrored what I had been thinking about New York fashion. And he had summed it up in one sentence. He'd seen straight through the New Yorker in me to who I really was.

And somehow, it irritated me. If I wanted to succeed, this was what I needed to do and who I needed to be. The reminder didn't help anything.

"I don't take fashion advice from drunk businessmen as a rule."

Derek laughed. "Hey, asshole, leave my sister alone."

Ash just shrugged. "Beer in the fridge?"

I took a fortifying breath and headed into the one bedroom. The guys would have to share the living space. I had a couch that probably wasn't long enough for their limbs and an air mattress. I closed the door to my room and took another deep breath.

Ash Talmadge was in my apartment in the city. He was drunk and an asshole and getting over his now ex-girlfriend ... but he was here. I'd seen him a few times when I went home in the year and a half since I'd graduated from Parsons, but he'd never visited me here. While the circumstances were far from ideal, I couldn't help but be glad.

I changed out of my all-black work attire and ransacked my closet for something to wear. I finally gave in on a black minidress that I'd been working on off the clock. I really thought it would look better in a pale baby blue or a really soft pink, but I'd never sell anything in those colors here. So, I'd gone for the safety choice.

I grabbed a pair of black Louboutins that I'd snagged from a shoot and carried them out to my living room. Both guys had a beer in hand. They'd turned on *SportsCenter*—I wasn't even aware I had ESPN—and were watching some commentary on Florida State taking on Notre Dame tomorrow night.

"Fly all this way to watch sports on my tiny TV?"

Derek waved me away, but Ash turned to say something and stopped midway, his eyes going wide. He glanced back at Derek hastily before doing a double take. His eyes traveling up my long legs to the very short dress and then up to my face.

My cheeks heated at the appraising look. "Like it?" I turned in a slow circle. "I made it myself."

"It, uh, it looks great," Ash said, clearing his throat.

Derek gave him a sharp look before glancing up at me. "Yeah, it's nice, Mia. Where are we going tonight?"

"Whatever y'all are in the mood for."

"Alcohol," Ash said.

"Sure. Like a dive bar or a nightclub or art scene or …"

"Wherever you'd go."

"All right. Let's grab some dinner, so you two don't drown tonight."

Derek snapped off the TV, and I took them to a local Italian restaurant. A few of my friends were going to a nightclub around the corner. We met up with them, breezing past the line and inside.

Alyssa and Zoey had been my roommates through all four years of Parsons. Zoey's wife, Tara, had practically lived with us the last year. They'd gotten married over the summer at Tara's Long Island home. I'd taken Camden with me, which was the death of our already-broken relationship.

Derek and Alyssa hit it off right away, as I'd figured they would. He drew her out onto the dance floor, and we lost them almost immediately. Zoey and Tara were next until it was just me and Ash at the bar.

We'd ordered a round of tequila shots before

Wait for Always

everyone disappeared. And now, there were six shots in front of us.

"They need to come back for these," I yelled over the loud music.

Ash held his up. "Their loss."

I laughed. "You want to drink them all? I'll be toast after that."

"We had a big dinner."

Which was true, but probably beside the point. Still, I shrugged and lifted my shot. We clinked glasses and downed the first round. I sucked on a lime while Ash downed a second shot and then a third.

My eyes rounded. "Whoa, whoa ... slow down."

"There. Now, you only have to take one more."

"Ash ..." I muttered softly.

He must have heard the sympathy in my voice because he shook his head and scooted the tequila over to me. So, he didn't want to talk. Fine. We'd just drink then. I raised my glass, and we downed the last round. I sucked on the lime, again wincing as the liquid burned down my throat.

"Come on," Ash said, taking my hand and pulling me out onto the dance floor.

We found the rest of my friends in the crowd. The tequila loosened up my entire body, and I fell into Ash's arms, dancing without reservation. For a few short hours, I forgot why he was here and what had happened to him. I forgot everything. Just laughed and danced and drank the night away.

Ash and I practically had to carry Derek back to the apartment. We looked ridiculous, hauling an enormous basketball player through the streets of New York. Luckily, my apartment wasn't far, and we threw him down on the couch, where he promptly passed out.

"Shit," I muttered. "I didn't blow up the air mattress."

I stumbled into my bedroom and rummaged through the top of my closet to locate it. I felt Ash's presence at my back more than heard it.

"Why don't I just stay in here?" he said.

I'd kicked off my heels, and suddenly, he was a good head taller than me. I swallowed, immediately sober at the suggestion. My body hummed with all the need I always felt for Ash Talmadge. But that ... that couldn't be what he was interested in.

"Here?" I whispered.

"You have a king-size bed," he said.

"Right. Uh ... sure."

He shot me a smirk and brushed my loose hair out of my eyes. "As long as you're okay with that?"

My heart stuttered. "It's fine with me. I'll just ... I'll just change."

I hustled into the bathroom and removed my dress. I pulled on a pair of sleep shorts and a sweatshirt. October was my favorite month in the city, but it was cold and drafty at night.

Ash had stripped down to his boxers and was

currently lying under the covers. I stumbled slightly at the sight of his muscled chest ... in my bed.

His eyes tracked me as I walked around to the other side and got into bed.

"I ... might have had too much to drink."

He laughed. "Derek had too much."

"Fair."

When he didn't say anything else, I leaned over and switched off the light. "Well ... good night."

"Good night, Mia."

But I couldn't sleep. I could feel his heat, even across the giant bed. I wanted to roll over and change everything in that moment. But he didn't want that. He never really had. And it wasn't fair to want that when he had just gone through a big break up.

"Amelia," he whispered into the dark.

"Yeah?"

"Thanks for having us for the weekend."

"Anytime." I swallowed and pushed forward. "You know you can talk to me if you want. If you need to talk about it."

Ash nodded. "Yeah, I know."

"Good."

A few minutes later, he said, "I want to forget that it ever happened."

"That's how I felt after Camden and I broke up."

Ash's eyes snapped up to mine. "You broke up?"

"Yeah. This summer."

"What happened?"

"You were right about him. He was an asshole."

"Sounds right."

I sighed. I didn't talk about Camden much either, but it was nice to have someone who cared. "I took him to Zoey and Tara's wedding. And he was just ... so judgmental."

"About them being together?"

"Actually, no. That would have been unforgivable. But he didn't care that they were lesbians, just that they weren't ... rich. And the crazy part is, they *are*. Tara's parents are surgeons. Zoey's dad is an investment banker in Boston."

"But it wasn't good enough for him."

"No, not like the money he's used to. He was a dick at the wedding, and then when I called him out on it, he ended it. Said we'd just been having fun anyway." I sighed. "I always got the impression that I was more serious about it than he was ... like I didn't quite fit. But it was so *easy* for him to leave me and go back to his Upper East Side friends and not care."

Ash inhaled sharply. "Yeah, they make it look so easy, don't they?"

I hesitated before responding, "Did Lila make it seem easy?"

He didn't say anything for a minute. "She did. She slept with someone else. Her ex."

I winced. "Jesus, Ash."

"You know ... I was willing to forgive her. I thought we'd be able to move past it."

"Why?" I gasped. "Why would you think that?"

"Because I love her."

"You don't deserve that."

"Well, she left anyway. And I'm not even mad at her, you know? Like, I just wonder if she went back to him. Back to Cole." He spoke that name as if it were acid.

"So what if she did?" I said, reaching across the bed and taking his hand. "She hurt you. She broke your trust. That isn't love, Ash."

He closed his eyes against those words. "Maybe you're right." He cleared his throat. "We should ... we should get some sleep."

He slid his hand out of mine and rolled over with his back to me. I wanted to reach for him, to comfort him in some way. I'd said what I believed, but it had clearly been the wrong thing. Too soon to tell him the truth and not just console him. Even if he deserved to hear it.

Also too soon for him to hear the truth that I'd kept to myself all these years. At least that one stayed locked behind my lips.

8

NEW YORK CITY
OCTOBER 20, 2014

Derek left Sunday afternoon to be back at work on Monday morning. Ash's flight wasn't until Tuesday morning. He hadn't said another word about Lila since Friday night, when he'd confessed to what had happened with her. But we both knew that he was staying longer so that he didn't have to return to reality. After what he'd told me, I hardly blamed him.

Before Derek had left, he'd hugged me and whispered, "Take care of him."

I'd promised that I would.

Not that I knew how to take care of Ash. He'd been drunk day and night since he had gotten here. Maybe he didn't even remember telling me about Lila.

"You have work today?" Ash asked the first morning we were alone in my apartment.

Wait for Always

"No, I took today off too."

"Really? Why?"

"You're here," I said like it was obvious.

"I would have been fine. I could have found a bar," he said, waving a hand dismissively.

"No day-drinking today," I told him. "We're going out."

He shot me an exasperated look. "I can day-drink if I want."

"Not today though. Get dressed. I'm showing you around the city."

I didn't wait for his response. But when I looked through my closet full of black work attire, I decided against it. I pushed to the back of the closet and pulled on jeans and a pink sweater with fashion sneakers. It was still fashionable, but not on the caliber that I'd been wearing the last couple of years. Camden certainly would have wrinkled his nose at it. But I looked cute and, most importantly, comfortable and in color.

When I came back out, my hair left to curl at the edges with only light makeup, Ash brightened considerably. "There's the Amelia Ballentine I know."

I laughed and shoved his shoulder. "Shut up."

He'd changed into khakis and a blue polo that matched his bright blue eyes. He looked gorgeous, and it took everything in me not to show that on my face.

"So ... where are we going?" he asked.

"I told you, I'm showing you my city."

He just smiled and followed me out of the apartment. We walked to Washington Square Park, grabbing bagels for breakfast from a local food truck. We strolled through the Strand's eighteen miles of books before heading north toward Union Square. We backtracked through the few blocks that housed The New School, and I showed him the fashion on display outside of Parsons. Then, we took the subway north to Madison Avenue, where we walked the immaculate line of fashion boutiques, which had been my dream for as long as I could remember.

"This is you?" he asked as we stopped in front of the Elizabeth Cunningham entrance.

"This is me."

A part of me was terrified to be seen in what I was wearing by someone at my job. I was supposed to represent them at all times. But maybe since I was dressed this down, no one would even recognize me.

"Did you design any of these?" he asked, pointing at the clothing in the window.

I shook my head. "I'm not that high up yet. I'm working underneath other designers and helping with strategies. Not quite getting coffee, but just above that."

He laughed. "I see. Sounds glamorous."

"It can be, but most of the time, it's a lot of hard work."

"But you love it?" he asked as he strolled toward Central Park.

"Most of the time."

"What about the times that you don't?"

"Well, it would be nice to be designing my own clothes. I've always wanted my own boutique. My own name on a store, you know?"

Ash nodded encouragingly. "You could do that."

I laughed. "I'm so far from being able to do that. I'm still trying to come up with my own unique brand that would make it worthwhile to branch out. Not to mention, I'd need the capital to start something like that."

"*This* feels more like your own unique brand," he said, gesturing to my clothes.

We wound through the park. The leaves had changed colors, and the oranges, reds, and yellows made the entire park come alive. I loved this time of year right before everything succumbed to winter's chill.

"Well, Southern doesn't really work here," I said with a laugh.

"Then, do it in the South."

"Maybe one day."

I couldn't deny that I'd thought about it. I loved New York. I loved high-end fashion. But I didn't exactly *belong* here. Not the way I did back home. I was constantly fighting my instincts and designing clothes I thought New York would like, but not necessarily what I loved.

"Wait ... wait right here," Ash said.

I furrowed my brow at him as he jogged away. We'd just reached Bethesda Fountain, and I stood at the center of it, all alone. A moment later, he was walking back over, holding something behind his back.

"What did you do?" I asked with a laugh.

He held out a red rose. "Your favorite, right?"

I took the rose from his hand in surprise. That he'd bought it for me. That he'd remembered at all. "Yes," I whispered. "Yes, they're my favorite. Classic."

"I thought so," he said, and we walked over to the edge of the water.

My heart was still in my throat. It hadn't been romantic ... and yet it was *so* romantic. It was so Ash. Anyone who had ever let him go was a total idiot.

"So, what do you want to do tonight?" he asked. "No drinking?"

I grinned. "I know this comedy show. I heard it's amazing. I always want to go, but weekdays are hard."

"I'm in."

Neither of us stuck to the *no drink* rule. I was having too good of a time at the show. I laughed until my cheeks hurt and my belly ached. The female performer was so good that she got a standing ovation from the crowd. There were three performers total, and she was the last. I could see why.

Wait for Always

As Ash and I stumbled out of the comedy show late that evening, we were both still cracking up at all the jokes. Recounting the best ones and dissolving into laughter again.

"One more drink?" he asked. "I'm not ready for the night to end."

And neither was I. I'd never be ready for my time with Ash to end.

"There's a bunch of bars around here. A martini bar in a hotel. A dive bar that Zoey always recommends. Um ..." I said, blanking on what else was nearby. "Or we can grab some wine and drink at my place."

"You know what? Let's go for the latter."

"Really?" I asked in surprise.

"Yeah. It's close, right?"

I nodded, and we headed back toward my place on Cornelia Street. We grabbed two bottles of wine from the liquor store and went upstairs. I tossed Ash the bottle opener as I dug around in my fridge.

"I think there's still part of that charcuterie board here. Or did y'all destroy it?"

"Um ... maybe," Ash said with a laugh.

"Fuck it. There's cheese still."

I grabbed the cubed cheese and brought it out to the living room, kicking off the heels I'd worn to the show. I dropped the cheese onto the table and then opened my old record player. Mom had gotten it for me last year for my birthday, and I'd been collecting records ever since. I set down an old Sinatra record, and "The Way You Look Tonight" filtered out of the player.

"I love this song," Ash said, popping the cork and pouring us each a glass.

I took the glass and flopped down onto the couch next to him, my mini dress riding up high on my thighs. Ash's eyes dipped down to my legs and then back up.

"I had a great day," Ash said.

"Me too."

"Even though we drank?"

"Well, we didn't drink until the show."

"I remember. I had a headache half the day."

I laughed. "Poor baby."

He laughed with me. "No, I mean it. This was nice. It was exactly what I needed. Just a day off to not think about anything."

"I'm glad."

Ash set his empty wine glass down on the coffee table, stood, and offered me his hand. "Can I have this dance?"

I sipped my wine. "You're serious? My apartment is too small."

He took my hand and pulled me to my feet. "Then, I'll have to hold you close."

He set my drink on the table and took my arms in his, and the waltz came back to us as if we'd never lost it. I remembered the exact weight of his arms, as we'd done this dance in front of hundreds of people at my debutante ball. It felt like so much more now. Nothing official about how far we were supposed to be separated, and he pulled me in close enough that our chests were nearly touching. When I looked up at him, I could have stood on tiptoe and met his lips.

I felt dizzy with the alcohol and his nearness as we moved to Sinatra. Everything fell away. The world belonged to us in that moment.

The song came to a crescendo. Ash spun me in a circle once, drew me into his arms, and then dipped me. I laughed softly as my head nearly touched the sofa. My apartment really was tiny. But it didn't matter because I was in Ash's arms. And he held me as if I was precious. And I wanted everything with this man. Everything.

Ash looked at me as if seeing me for the first time. He pulled me back to my feet. The music was still playing, but we weren't moving. He tilted my head up to look at him.

"Please," I whispered as our bodies touched. The alcohol made me bold enough to ask for what I wanted.

"Amelia," he groaned.

Then, his lips crashed down onto mine. This was nothing like our first kiss, which had been slow and sensual and built up in my mind as the best kiss of my entire life. But I'd been just eighteen then, and this was something utterly different. This was ecstasy.

Our lips moved together, saying all the things I'd wanted to say for years. Saying everything with that one kiss. That I was his. Utterly and completely. And I didn't care what happened, but I wanted this tonight. I wanted him. I'd always wanted him.

His other arm snaked around my waist and dragged me hard against him. Our bodies crushed together until there was barely room to breathe.

At the first sweep of his tongue, a moan escaped me. He smiled against my mouth, clearly enjoying how much *I* was enjoying him. And then he delved in, caressing my tongue with his. Shivers ran down my body and need pulsed through me.

"Oh," I said as he nipped at my bottom lip.

His hand ran down my side, feeling his way over the curve of my waist before pushing back up until he found my breast. I was still in the skimpy black dress I'd worn to the show. I'd skipped a bra, and he must have noticed. Because he growled deep in the back of his throat as his hand cupped my breast. His fingers flicked against my nipple, making me shudder against him.

He released my mouth, working his way to my ear and then down the column of my throat. I tilted back to give him better access as I gripped on to the front of his button-up. He reached my collarbone, pushed my strap off of my shoulder, and kissed across it.

"Mia, Mia, Mia," he purred against my skin.

"Yes," I gasped.

His hands moved to my ass, and then, suddenly, he was hoisting me into the air. I wrapped my arms around his neck as he started to walk out of the living room. He toed the door open. He'd slept in here the first night he was here, but he hadn't been back inside since.

He dropped me onto the bed, covering my body with his and returning those beautiful lips to mine. I hadn't released him with my legs, and I could feel exactly what our kissing had done to him as well.

I reached a hand between us and brushed against his dick. He groaned deep in the back of his throat as he pushed himself into my hand.

"Amelia," he groaned.

I gripped him tighter through his pants. Fuck, I wanted him out of these pants. My hands moved to his belt, yanking it free. I popped the button and dragged the zipper down. Then, I pushed my hand into his boxers and slid my hand around the hard length of him.

"Jesus Christ," he groaned. His head dipped into my shoulder as I stroked him. "Fucking hell."

I rolled him over and straddled his hips. I moved my body down the length of him, taking his pants and boxers with me. At the first touch of my mouth to his cock, he moaned. It was the best sound I'd ever heard. I wasn't ashamed to say that I'd dreamed of doing this. It wasn't that I loved giving head, but I knew I was good at it. And I wanted Ash to feel good. I wanted him to feel as good as I did, just being around him.

I bobbed up and down on him, running my hand down the shaft until he got longer and harder in my mouth. He was already as big as I'd imagined ... all those times I'd seen him in swim trunks at the beach.

I could tell he was getting close by the way he gripped my hair and forced me down harder. He wasn't going to last another couple minutes as far as I was concerned.

But then, suddenly, he stopped me. "Not ready."

"What?" I asked in confusion. What guy stopped himself from coming in a girl's mouth?

He rolled me back over and tugged his button-up over his head before stripping me of my dress. I was in nothing but a thong, which he pulled aside as he slipped a finger inside of me.

I gasped. I was soaking wet. *Soaked through my thong* wet.

"Oh, that turns you on," he said before slipping a second finger inside of me.

"You," I told him. I was seeing stars. "You do."

"Condom?" he asked.

I pointed to the drawer next to my bed. He removed his fingers, leaving me a panting mess on the bed as he sheathed himself. Then, he maneuvered himself between my legs, lifting one to his hip. The tip of his cock was pressed against my opening. I shifted forward, wanting nothing more than to have him inside of me.

"You're sure?" he still managed to ask even though we were naked and wet and poised at the edge of a precipice.

"Yes," I said. "Yes, I want this."

Then, he thrust forward, and he was inside of me. I cried out something incoherent at the first feel of him. His hands were bruisingly hard on my hips as he pulled out and slammed back inside. I drew him down to me. Chest to chest. Lips to lips. I wanted nothing between us. Nothing but this moment.

Our rhythm picked up as we learned the sway of each other's bodies. Two magnets finding their way back again and again. Completing a pairing that made me dizzy with desire. Like this would never ever be enough.

I'd dreamed of being with Ash Talmadge. I was embarrassed at how many times I'd gotten myself off at the thought of him. And now, here he was, pushing me to come with his mouth and hands and cock. It was better than I'd ever imagined. Sweaty and sticky and delicious. Real. So very real.

He grunted as the only warning before he followed me over the edge, and then we were both crying out as the orgasm took us. His body went limp at the end of it. The only sounds were our panting and the city noises beyond.

He pressed a kiss to my temple before sliding out of

me and heading into the bathroom. For a second, as I lay naked on my bed, I worried that I'd wake up and this would all be a dream again. But Ash returned to me with a smile, drawing me against him and falling asleep with me in his arms.

I didn't dream that night.

Nothing could compare to reality.

9

NEW YORK CITY
OCTOBER 21, 2014

*A*sh wasn't in bed when I woke up.

I stretched my arm overhead and rolled over with a yawn. Light streamed in through the windows, city noise filtered inside, and the sheets were a tangle around my bare legs. I'd pulled my sweatshirt on at some point in the night. I reached for my shorts as I kicked my legs over the bed. I was halfway to the bedroom door when Ash appeared in the doorframe.

"Morning," I said with a bright smile.

Last night ran through my mind like a movie. It had been ... perfect. Better than I'd ever thought it would be. And now, I just wanted to keep him here forever.

I stepped forward to give him a kiss, but he put his hand out to stop me.

"Amelia."

That was when I realized he wasn't smiling. In fact,

he seemed as aloof and broody as I'd ever seen him. His hair was messy, as if he'd been running his hands through it. His eyes were downcast.

"What is it?"

"Last night ..."

I gulped. "What about it?"

He sighed heavily. "It shouldn't have happened."

"What?" I whispered in disbelief.

I suddenly felt like an animal caught in a trap. Frantic and desperate to get away. I couldn't have this conversation. I couldn't ruin the best moment of my life with whatever he was about to say. And yet I couldn't leave. I couldn't walk away from my own horror show.

"I mean, it was good," he said. As if *that* were the problem. "That's not what I meant. It just ... it shouldn't have happened. We were drunk, and I'd just gone through a breakup. I'm sorry. I shouldn't have taken advantage of you like that."

Taken advantage of *me*.

He thought he'd taken advantage of me.

When I'd wanted this to be my reality for my whole life.

"That isn't what happened," I said quickly.

He winced. "It is. We'd had a good day, and I was so fucked up. You were ... here."

I was here.

He didn't feel the way I did. Of course he didn't. I'd known that, and yet I'd still fallen into bed with him. I'd let myself believe that he wanted this like I did.

No, worse. I hadn't cared why he wanted me. I'd given in to that base desire within me that said I'd do anything to have Ash. For any reason. Any reason at all. And he had last night.

Now, in the daylight, it was all clear that this was a rebound. I was a rebound for Ash. Lila had slept with Cole. And so he'd slept with me. To make himself feel better or something.

I felt like I was going to be sick.

And I couldn't do that. I couldn't let him see that on me. I hadn't seen past my own desires to what was reality. If I'd known it was a rebound, would I still have done it? Yes. Would it have hurt a little less? Maybe. But I hadn't realized. And now, it felt like my heart was being ripped from my chest.

"And Derek," Ash said with another wince. "Fuck, Derek can't know."

I nodded vigorously. "Right. Derek. No, I won't tell Derek."

"Amelia, I'm sorry. I really am."

"What are you sorry for?" I asked with a soft laugh.

I reached deep down inside of me for that pageant smile. One that I'd never had to use with Ash. He could normally see it for what it was, but he must not have wanted to look for it right now. He must have wanted so badly for me to be fine with this that he didn't care.

"You're not ... upset?"

"No," I lied. "It's fine, Ash. We had fun, right?"

"Yeah. I mean, of course we did."

I took a step backward and kept that fake smile up. "You're going through a lot. Don't worry about me."

"I shouldn't have taken advantage of you." He ran his hand back through his hair again. "You're my best friend's little sister. And you're such a good friend."

"Please stop saying that. You didn't take advantage of me. I was a willing participant," I reminded him. "I said yes. I said yes many times."

His cheeks tinted pink at my words, and he cleared his throat. "Right. Yeah, you did."

"So, uh ... just don't worry about it," I told him, sidling past him. "It was a one-time thing."

Ash hastily moved out of my way, as if touching me would set off a land mine. "Sure. One-time thing. I don't want this to change anything between us."

"Of course not." I reached for the bathroom door. "Just going to take a shower. Have to get into work after you leave for the airport."

"Okay," he said, taking another step back.

I entered the bathroom, turned the shower up as hot as it would go, and then slumped to the ground with my back to the door. I waited for his retreating steps before I let my smile drop, and the tears hit me. I put my face into my hands and cried like I hadn't since Camden had dumped me. Maybe not even then.

I'd been an idiot. A complete and total fool. I had wanted this so badly that I'd given up my entire heart for that moment. For a moment that he didn't want anyone to know about, that he never wanted to talk about again.

My heart cracked straight down the middle, as if Ash had taken a chisel and split it in half. I was just a little girl again, mooning over her brother's best friend. All I'd wanted was for him to notice me. The boy I'd always had a crush on. Now, he had. Now, he'd had me. And it hadn't been enough.

No. Worse. It had been nothing.

A good time. A one-night stand. A rebound.

I cried harder at that word. I cried until I had no more tears left in me. Until I felt numb to the pain of a broken heart.

Then, I swiped at my eyes, pulled myself up, and looked into the foggy mirror. I wiped my hand across the glass to look at my blurry reflection in the surface. The girl looking back at me was nothing like the woman I wanted to be.

Maybe this was how first love died.

With the loss of innocence.

PART II

10

SAVANNAH
PRESENT

"Amelia, are we out of those green dresses?" Sasha raced across the shop to where I was currently working the second cash register.

"The ones with the puff sleeves and square neck?"

"That's the one," Sasha said.

The customer tapped their credit card, and I passed her the black-and-gold Ballentine bag. "Thanks!" she said excitedly. "I'm going to wear this tonight."

"Have a nice day!" I called back. I turned back to Sasha. "I think we only have it in pink still. The green went so fast, even before St. Patrick's Day."

St. Patrick's Day was an entire *event* in Savannah. It had the one of the largest parades in the entire country, only second to New York City, and the parade went right past my shop on Broughton. Upward of four hundred thousand people came into our small town for the entire week surrounding the event. It was single-handedly our busiest week of the year. I'd ordered more stock than ever, and still, the store was nearly bare bones already with one more day left of the madness.

"Next year, twice as many green dresses," Sasha said with a laugh.

"I ordered twice as many as the last St. Patrick's Day. It's been nuts." I shrugged. "Hold down the register, and I can look in the back."

Sasha took over, taking the next customer's apparel.

I rummaged through our back stock, looking for anything else green. The puff sleeves were all the rage this season. I'd seen girls all over town, wearing my brightly colored attire with lace and big sleeves and sheer fabric and all the things New York had scoffed at me for. They all worked here in the South, and even better, my name was on the building.

I overturned another box and gasped when I found a whole *box* of the green dresses secreted away. Well, well, well, these were going to go like televisions on Black Friday.

"We're in luck," I told Sasha as I came back, hefting the box in my arms.

My stepmom Kathy rushed over when she saw me under the box. "Sweetheart, let me get that."

Kathy usually sat on boards and ran charities and that sort of work. But when the store was busy, she

Wait for Always

always dropped in and took an all-day shift to help out. When I told her that she didn't have to, she always reminded me that she was too proud of me not to put in some work herself.

"These need to get on hangers. Also, Sasha, what size did the girl need?"

"I think a small. It was in the room for Calli."

I snagged a small from the box and walked over to the dressing rooms. There was a line seven people back. I hung the dress on the hanger outside of Calli's dressing room.

"Here's that small in green, Calli."

"Oh my God, thank you so much." She came out, wearing a pink-and-purple strapless dress with tie-up ruched sides.

"That looks amazing on you."

"I love all your clothes," she gushed.

"Me too," a voice said behind her.

I whipped around and gasped. "Josie!"

Whispers started all around us. Josephine Reynolds was a local celebrity. She'd done seven seasons of the hit show *Academy* and recently a full-length movie for it. Not to mention, the film she'd just directed and starred in, *Montgomery House*, which was winning *all* the awards. She was also a close friend. We'd gotten to know each other when I was working at Elizabeth Cunningham. I designed dresses for her Emmy events, and we'd hit it off.

Sometimes, it was still weird to me that my sister-in-law, Marley, and one of my closest friends, Josie, were also Lila's best friends since childhood. It shouldn't be possible that we loved all the same people when I still thought of her as the girl who had broken Ash's heart.

"Come to the back before you get mobbed," I said with a laugh.

"I won't get mobbed. I can handle my fame."

But she followed me out of the store and into the back room.

"I forgot how crazy it gets for St. Patrick's," Josie said. "I was coming by to see if you'd made progress on the dress, but I'm going to guess no."

Josie was getting married in a few months to Maddox Nelson, Marley's twin brother. She'd asked me to design the wedding dress even though I'd never done that sort of work before. I was up for the challenge though. How different was it really from a pageant dress?

"I haven't touched it since you last saw it. Don't worry though, it'll be ready in time."

"I have no fear. We should get lunch sometime."

"Absolutely. Once the tourists leave, I am there."

"How have you been holding up since you and Mark broke up?" Josie asked.

I shrugged. "I had to go and get a box from his house, and it was a nightmare."

"Fuck that guy."

"Thanks," I said with a laugh.

Wait for Always

I bit my lip. I knew exactly what Josie thought about Ash Talmadge. But I hadn't told anyone about our date, except Marina, who was too far away. It would be nice to have someone to talk about it in person.

"I actually have a date tonight."

"Really?" she gasped. "Tell me all the details. Who is the lucky guy?"

I looked down at my feet. "Well, he's a mutual friend. Erm ... of sorts."

Josie grabbed my arm. "You're joking! *James*?"

Josie was the only person I knew who called Ash by his first name. It had always seemed out of general animosity, but lately, maybe there was some affection to it.

"Yeah. Ash asked me out. Well, he'd been asking me out for, like, a week, and I kept turning him down. I don't know ... it feels different this time."

"Like a real date? Not that bullshit y'all were trying to feed all of us that you were just friends?"

"A real date," I confirmed.

"I thought you weren't going to do anything with him until he was ... over Lila," Josie said softly. "I thought after what happened at my party ..."

"That was last year and Lila is marrying Cole. Can't get much more over her."

Josie arched an eyebrow. "We both know that isn't true."

"Look, I know you don't like him."

"That's not true," Josie interjected. "I don't like him with Lila."

I coughed not so subtly. "Same."

"I've made my fair share of relationship mistakes. But Ash is different with you, Amelia. He was long before he could admit it to himself," she said gently. "I just don't want to see you get hurt."

"I don't want that either." I bit my lip. "Is it too much to hope that he'll pick me after all this time? Am I an idiot for giving him another chance?"

"You've loved him your whole life. Give him a fair shot. If it doesn't work out, then you'll know, and you can move on if you have to."

I nodded. Josie was right. I'd spent a lot of time stressing about making the right choice around Ash. I didn't want to be the same dumb girl, too interested in being with him without taking into consideration how he felt. Now, I knew. I'd been that girl, and I wouldn't be again.

This was our shot.

If I was ever going to find out if this would work, then I had to put myself out there again. Which was the hardest part of all.

11

SAVANNAH
PRESENT

By the time we closed the shop for the day, everyone was exhausted, and our shelves were nearly empty.

"What are we even going to sell tomorrow?" Sasha asked, lounging back on the couch in the back room.

Kathy gestured to the small number of boxes. "Someone should probably put these out."

I'd gotten some more inventory in this morning, but we hadn't had an extra set of hands all day to open them and get them on the shelves.

"Not tonight," I told them. "I can come in early and do it. Thanks for all your help."

Kathy kissed my cheek and offered to show up early tomorrow to help too. I couldn't say no even if she would have let me. I needed the help.

Sasha gave me a hug before heading out, but Kathy stayed behind for a minute.

"Everything okay?"

"I'm so proud of you, honey."

I beamed. "Thanks."

"Maybe you could come over to the house sometime soon for dinner."

"Oh." I should have seen it coming. Kathy tried to play mediator between me and Dad all the time. "I think I'm busy."

"Your father wants to spend time with you."

"Then, he could come himself," I said snappishly.

Kathy sighed. "One day, you two are going to have to work this out."

I shrugged. "I'll put in exactly as much effort as he does."

Kathy nodded, seeing that she'd lost again, because my dad didn't put in any effort. She hugged and wished me good-bye, leaving me all alone in my shop.

I flopped down at my desk with a sigh. What a mess. And not one I felt like I had to clean up. Parents sometimes had to deal with the consequences of their actions too.

My phone dinged, and I grabbed it to see a text from Marina.

Have fun on your date tonight.

Thanks! Nervous and excited.

Don't put out.

I snorted. *Oh, Marina.*

Not in the plan, but thanks ... I think.

Tell him I'll kill him if he hurts you.

I think Derek would handle him.

> *True, true. But I want it to go amazing! I want it to go so well that you bring him with you to Charleston in a few weeks and you're drunk on love.*

I smiled at that image. Ash used to go to Charleston with us all the time. It wouldn't be strange to bring him with me. Except that I was planning to leave and not take him with me.

We'll see. It's a first date. I'm not getting my hopes up.

Too late. We both know you're already a goner.

And damn, wasn't that true?

I sighed and tossed my phone back into my purse. I stripped out of the green pants and white puff-sleeve top I'd been wearing all day. I rummaged through the closet I had of my pieces in development and withdrew a pink satin dress that fell to mid-thigh and hugged my curves in all the right places. My hair was still in the high pony I'd put it in this morning with little wisps framing my face. I reapplied a coat of pink lipstick and called it good enough. I didn't have time to go home if we were going to make our reservation.

Still, I didn't hurry through the store. I walked fondly through it, running my hand over the few racks of dresses, noting what was selling out and what was still here. Cataloging what would work for next season and what I'd scrap. All my career dreams were in this building. It felt good to see all my hard work pay off.

I crossed the street to my BMW and got behind the wheel. Ash's house wasn't far from the store. He lived in a Victorian downtown that was much too big for him. My place was smaller. A townhouse away from all the tourists. But Ash had always liked to be in the thick of it.

All the parking was gone by the time I got over to his house. I circled the block three times before parking a few streets over. Damn tourists.

The walk was well lit, and with so many people on the street, it didn't feel unsafe for once, being a woman, alone. I jogged up the few steps to the front door of Ash's house and knocked twice.

I waited a few seconds before the door cracked open. Ash's smiling face greeted me. He was in khakis and a button-up, rolled up to his elbows. No jacket. No tie. The first two buttons were undone at his throat. His hair was gelled to perfection, and those blue eyes were all for me. I could barely breathe at the sight of him.

"Hey," I muttered.

Wait for Always

"Hey. Come on in."

"Aren't we going to be late for our reservation?" I asked but followed him into the house.

He closed the door behind me and gave me a bedazzling smile. "I might have canceled our reservation."

"What? Why?" I checked the time and winced. "I'm not that late."

"You're not late at all, but it felt like a lot after the week you've had. I didn't want to put more on you. I thought we could do something else instead."

Dinner had felt ... uncomplicated. It had felt like an easy first step. We'd never done anything like that before, and I'd thought it would feel more like a normal relationship.

"But ... we can go out if you prefer," he said quickly. "I should have checked with you first. I just did this instead."

And that was when I realized there was music playing softly from the dining room. Music I recognized.

"Is that ... Sinatra?" I asked.

He grinned. "It's not a record, but I know you love old music."

"Classic music," I corrected.

"Right. Classics. Like red roses."

I looked at him in surprise, and he drew me through the living room and into the dining room. My mouth dropped open when I saw the table had been set for two with candlelight and red roses waiting in a vase.

"What's this?"

A timer dinged in the kitchen.

"Hold that thought. That's the potatoes."

I blinked. "Potatoes?"

Ash rushed into the kitchen and opened the oven. The smell of garlic filled the room. I breathed in deeply.

"Did you ... cook for me?"

"Technically, I grilled."

My heart soared. This was so ... not Ash. I hadn't even known he could cook. I knew he could use a grill, but he certainly never had for me before. Ash was the kind of guy who threw money around to show how he felt about people. He didn't set dinner to candlelight while playing Sinatra and cooking. But he had. For me.

"I have wine," he said, gesturing to an open bottle of red on the counter. "Help yourself."

I set my purse down on the island and poured each of us a glass of wine. Ash carried dinner to our place settings. I took the chair next to him at the table, still sort of shocked by everything happening. I'd thought I knew what to expect with Ash. I'd known him my entire life after all. But I'd been wrong. I liked being wrong.

"Is this okay?" he asked. "Next time, we can go out."

"No," I said quickly. "This is perfect."

Not only was it perfect, but the food was also delicious. The steak had a chimichurri sauce on top that made it succulent. The potatoes were well seasoned and *melt in your mouth* soft. There was even a crusty French bread.

"How was the store today?" he asked.

"Busy," I said with a head shake. "I have to go in early to restock. We're down to basically nothing on the shelves. I should have ordered more for this week, but I don't think I could have imagined what it was going to be like."

"That's great though."

"It is. It's great for the business."

"And for your meeting in Charleston. If it does it here, you can show that it would do it there."

"True," I said softly.

I hadn't considered what my numbers for this week would look like there. They didn't have the St. Patrick's Day crowds, but Charleston had its own events that brought in a lot of traffic. I could just see the girls all wearing my dresses on Folly Beach.

"I could get you a meeting with Nolan," Ash added easily.

I nearly choked on my drink. "With Nolan?"

"Yeah. You said you were already meeting with someone at Holden Holdings. Nolan and I are friends. I'm sure he'd meet with you."

"Nolan is, like ... buying up commercial real estate up and down the coast. I don't think he'd care about my one little clothing boutique."

"He would. I did."

"Yeah, but you know me."

He arched an eyebrow. "He's met you before."

"That's ... that's different."

"It really wouldn't be hard."

"I thought you didn't want me to go to Charleston."

He reached across the table and slid his hand over mine. "I don't want you to move there, but I would never stop you from following your dreams."

My heart wrenched in my chest at the statement. The words that I'd always wanted to hear. The man I'd always wanted him to be for me.

"Well, I guess I would appreciate it then. It's not necessary though. If it's too much trouble—"

"It's not," he said immediately.

This was how the world worked. Camden had gotten me that interview for Elizabeth Cunningham. I was old enough now to realize it wouldn't have happened without him. It didn't matter how good I was. His word was law. I could get the store in Charleston on my own. I knew what I was capable of now, but it would certainly be easier if Ash put in a good word for me.

When we finished dinner, I helped him clear our plates. We grabbed our wineglasses and headed into the backyard. Ash had a pool and a hot tub with an outdoor kitchen, and the whole thing was illuminated by Edison bulbs. I'd just set my glass down on a table when the song switched to "The Way You Look Tonight."

I laughed. "I always think of you when I hear this song."

"Me too."

Then, he took my hand in his and pulled me against him. I stopped breathing for a second as we moved effortlessly into the waltz. This was nothing like my deb ball and even less like that stupid night in New York City when I'd given myself over to him. This was the real Ash Talmadge. And he was only here for me.

He drew me closer, and I rested my head on his shoulder.

"Why is this so easy?" I asked.

"Because we fit, Mia."

A year ago, I would have killed for him to say those words. For him to finally get past his past and see me for me. Ash and I had always fit together, but that wasn't our reality. It never had been. No matter how easy it felt.

I pulled out of his arms. "I should probably go. Thank you for dinner."

He frowned. "You want to leave already?"

"It's been a long week."

"Stay," he said. He took my hand in his and brought it to his mouth. "Go swimming with me."

"Ash ..."

"Come on. It'll be fun. The hot tub is perfect in the spring."

I opened my mouth to object, but what came out was, "I don't have a suit."

"So?"

I laughed. "I'm not going in this dress. I just designed it. I don't even have it mapped out."

"So?" he repeated.

Then, he started to unbutton his shirt. My mouth went dry at every inch of his bare chest. He got to the bottom and then threw the shirt onto one of the chairs.

"Are you coming?" he asked as he popped the button on his khakis.

"Oh my God, Ash!"

He laughed as he kicked his shoes off. "What? We've been swimming together before."

"Yeah, but in bathing suits," I reminded him.

He dropped his khakis and tossed them on top of his shirt. "I'll turn around until you're in the water. Would that help?"

"I'm not embarrassed," I argued.

"Then, get in here," he said as he slid down into the steamy water.

I took a deep breath. I'd had an amazing night. I wasn't really ready to leave, but if I did this, where would it lead? Had Marina been onto something when she told me not to put out?

"Fuck it." I tugged the dress over my head and dropped it next to his pants. I was in nothing but a nude bra and lacy pink panties.

Ash had turned around even though I hadn't told

him to, and he didn't spin back around until he heard the splash of me getting into the hot tub. His eyes still went wide with desire at the sight of me in nothing but a bra.

"I can't believe you got me to do this. My hair is going to curl."

He grabbed my arm and drew me across the hot tub. "I like it when it curls."

"Curls are in right now at least. If only I had them like Marley, you know? Mine is more like a curl, wave, straight mix, as if it can't quite decide on a texture. That's why I always straighten it."

His hands slipped down my bare sides as I stood between his knees. "It's pretty however you wear it. You know that."

My hands moved to his chest. If he was going to touch me like that, I was going to get my fill too.

"Mia," he said, pulling me closer until our chests nearly touched, "I'm glad you came over."

"I thought about canceling."

"I'm glad you didn't."

His hands slid lower, picking me up easily in the water and settling me into his lap. I wrapped my arms around his neck.

"Marina told me not to put out."

Ash guffawed. "I see."

I realized just how little clothing was between us. I was in the smallest scrap of fabric. He could be inside of me in seconds if I let him. And a part of me really wanted it. The loudest part knew how bad of an idea it was to go this fast with him.

"And that she'd kill you if you hurt me."

"That seems to be going around," he said.

"Derek?"

He shrugged. "I told him we were going out so that he wouldn't find out secondhand."

"Yeah. I told Josie this afternoon."

His eyes flashed. "Really? What did the infamous Josephine Reynolds think?"

"That you're different with me."

His expression softened. "Well, she's not wrong."

I closed my eyes and sighed heavily. But he was there, drawing my face up to his.

"Hey," he said. "Look at me."

I slowly opened my eyes to meet his blue orbs. My heart ached for him. For the lost girl who had wanted nothing more than this. And the woman seated on his lap who needed so much more.

"How do I know you won't hurt me again?"

"Because your brother will kill me."

I laughed despite myself and swatted at him. "I'm being serious."

He arched an eyebrow. "So am I."

"Don't be an ass."

He grinned wickedly at me. "Look, all I know is that I couldn't look forward into my future for a long time. I was too bogged down in the past. And when I look forward now, all I see is you."

At those words, I let go. I let go of the pain of our shared past and decided to look at the future.

So, when he dipped his head to meet my lips, I didn't stop him. I leaned into it. The kiss was sweet like summer watermelon, memorable like a pageant win, and pure joy like twirling in a brand-new dress.

As much as I wanted it to go further than that, I didn't let it. Ash didn't push for me either. It was enough to be together. To make out in his hot tub and realize we had time to figure out where this was going.

So, we made plans for another date and another after that. And I let that hope creep back in, unbidden.

12

SAVANNAH
JULY 15, 2016

"Ballentine is the newest clothing store in downtown Savannah," the mayor of Savannah said joyously as he held a red ribbon in front of my store. "We're lucky to have the owner, Amelia Ballentine, here with us today for the official grand opening."

I beamed with a pair of enormous gold scissors in my hands. My whole family stood behind me. Mom had driven into Savannah with her latest boyfriend, Ian. Dad was on my other side with his arm around a proud Kathy. Derek and his fiancée, Kasey, stood between the two sides of our family. And me in the middle. I was so excited about today that I didn't even have time to stress about anything.

The mayor said a few more congratulatory words before gesturing for me to cut the ribbon, which I did. The crowd cheered. Reporters flashed their cameras. I smiled and waved like I was back in my pageant days.

Then, the ceremony was over, and my store was officially open.

We'd soft-launched two weeks ago. I sold out of half of my stock on the first day. I was terrified that I wouldn't be able to order enough extra to make the grand opening feel *grand*, but I worked my ass off to get here. I hadn't stopped then.

"We're so proud of you," Mom said, pulling me in for a hug.

"Thanks, Mom."

"I cannot wait to see everyone in all of your clothes all over Savannah," Kathy said.

My heart thudded at that thought. I'd imagined it, of course. But *seeing* it was going to be the best feeling in the whole wide world.

"Yeah, it's cool, I guess," Derek joked.

"You're such a dick," I said, punching him in the arm.

"Be nice to your sister," Kasey said with an eye roll. "Isn't he the worst?"

"I was kidding. I mean, you're a Ballentine. Our name is on the store. Can't be anything but excellent," Derek said.

"Ballentines are always excellent," Dad agreed.

I tried not to cringe. To hold on to the buoyant feeling I'd had all day. I was more than the sum of my parts. I'd put Ballentine on the store because it was a known entity. It was my last name. Amelia's just didn't sound as strong from a marketing standpoint. And yeah, I was proud of my last name. I'd reclaimed it from my father.

"But what am I wearing?" a voice called through the crowd.

My eyes widened and then snapped to my mom. "You didn't!"

She grinned. "I did."

And then my cousins were barreling through the crowd, heading right to me. Marina crashed into me first in cutoff jean shorts and a baseball shirt. Her hair was pulled back into a baseball cap.

"Rina, I missed you," I gasped.

She laughed. "I missed you too. Should have come to visit."

I gestured to the store. "Not enough time."

"Yeah, yeah."

"We're proud of you," Daron said. He was well over six feet tall with muscular football-player shoulders and a deep, dark tan from days spent out on the water, running the family business.

"Thanks, Dare." I gave him a hug and then turned to Tye for one as well. "I'm so glad you're here."

"Wouldn't have missed it," Tye said with a smile. He was shorter than Daron, and even though he had been adopted, they still looked alike. Dark tans and curls in their hair and wide, bright smiles. But Tye was the artist to Daron's athlete. Since Tye was the same

Wait for Always

age as me and Marina, we'd always run around together in the summers. Until he decided he wanted to be as cool as Daron and hanging out with two girls wasn't cool. It was around this same time that Tye had realized he was bi.

I ruffled his hair. "Didn't bring your boyfriend?"

He blushed and rolled his eyes. "He's flying this weekend."

"Ah, that pilot life," I said with a laugh.

Tye shrugged and started to explain the situation to Kathy. My dad's face pinched at the details. I wanted to hit him for it. Why even were men?

I had to get inside and work soon, but part of me had been waiting for one more person to complete the day. The one person who had helped me get prime real estate on Broughton for the shop. Except I didn't see Ash Talmadge anywhere.

And though I had let my old crush on him die for my own sanity, I couldn't help wishing.

Ash's parents were here. Mr. and Mrs. Talmadge had already come over to congratulate me. That had been nice. His mom was a bit ... neurotic, but despite the hundred-dollar curtain fiasco of our childhood, she'd always liked me. Probably because I'd done all the "right" things. I had the right family name. The right debutante ball. The right pageants. All of that. The only thing that could make me better in her eyes was for me to quit working entirely and get married to someone respectable.

"All right," I said, giving up on Ash showing up for me ... even though he always had in the past. "I should head inside. There's already a line!"

Everyone wished me luck. Derek insisted we go out after I closed. And then it was just me trekking into the shop to work for the day.

My newest cashier, Sasha, seemed to be the best of the lot. I could definitely see her moving up in the company if she kept at it.

"So exciting," she gushed.

I laughed. "It really is."

"But, oh my God, look at that hottie with *flowers* at the entrance."

"Who even says hottie anymore, Sasha?"

She laughed, but I followed her gaze to the front door. And damn it, there was the most gorgeous man I'd ever seen in my entire life, holding a bouquet of red roses.

"Hold down the fort," I said as a wide smile hit my face.

"Your boyfriend?" she guessed.

"Just a friend."

"My friends don't bring me red roses, looking that hot," she muttered under her breath.

I laughed and walked over to Ash. "You made it!"

"Sorry I missed the big opening ceremony," he said, passing me the roses and pulling me in for a quick hug.

"It's okay. It was boring anyway. Your parents were there."

"Ah, fun times," he said. "Was Mom ... okay?"

"You know how she is. She asked why I wasn't already married."

He shook his head. "She's very traditional."

"That's a word for it." I bit my lip. "What kept you?"

"A meeting ran over. But I wanted to drop these off for you."

"Thanks. Derek said we were going to go out tonight to celebrate. Marina, Daron, and Tye are in town. You coming?"

"Of course. I'll see you tonight then," he said with that same smile that always drew me in.

I tried to keep my heart in check. To remember that he didn't see me that way. He never really had. He was just a friend who had been there for me when I moved home.

In fact, he was half the reason I'd pulled the trigger.

I'd been working for Elizabeth Cunningham for almost three years when I finally said *fuck it* and designed something else, something more me. Elizabeth herself stormed into my office and chewed me out for the "catastrophe" I had designed. We got into it, screaming at each other until she fired me. I'd scooped up all my designs and walked out of the office with my head held high.

Every single one of those dresses was already a best seller in my new shop, and I didn't regret a damn thing. But after the adrenaline had run out, I'd been terrified, and I'd called Ash to see if he was serious about helping me find a store to open in Savannah. We'd worked it all out in the following months until my lease ran out and I moved home to open Ballentine.

But it had always been professional. Friends at best.

"Hey, I have something I want to talk to you about later," he said, his smile turning soft at the edges.

"Oh?" I asked, trying to keep the hope out of my voice.

"Not now. Let's talk about it when we go out, okay?"

"Sure. Everything okay?"

"Of course. I just ... I need to talk to you."

My heart pattered traitorously in my chest. "Okay, Ash. I'll see you tonight."

He beamed. "Tonight. Bye, Mia."

Clutching the red roses, I watched him go and wondered what the hell he was going to tell me. It was stupid to hope that he'd finally realized his feelings for me. I shouldn't even want that after what had happened in New York City. That probably wasn't what it was about anyway.

That was just what I obsessed about all day on my first day of work.

Marina looped her arm with mine as we walked through City Market downtown. The sun was setting on the horizon. It felt like it was later and later each night. So late that for the Fourth, we'd waited until nearly ten to set off fireworks. But I loved it. I loved summer and all the possibilities it always seemed to herald.

Derek and Kasey had gone on to Lulu's Chocolate Bar to stake a big enough table for the lot of us. Daron and Tye were trailing behind us, eating a caramel apple. They turned into children when they came back to Savannah during the summer. Ash was supposed to be meeting us at Lulu's. Anticipation clawed up my throat.

"So, what do you think he's going to say?" Marina asked excitedly.

I shrugged. "Could be anything."

"Do you think he's going to ask you out?"

"Why wouldn't he have done that at the shop?"

Marina had ditched her baseball cap and jean shorts for one of my dresses. A bright purple number that popped against her deep tan. Her long, silky, dark hair fell like a sheet down her back. We could have been sisters instead of cousins today, and I liked it better that way.

"He wouldn't want to ask you at your work!"

"Maybe," I said uncertainly.

"I bet it's that. I bet he wants to ask you out somewhere not related to work."

"I'll wait and see. Let's not get my hopes up." It was already too late. "Tell me about the guy you're seeing."

Marina sighed heavily. "Nolan's a dick. Let's not talk about him."

I snorted. "Then, why are you seeing him if he's a dick?"

Marina shot me a dirty look, and I burst out laughing.

She winked at me. "He's just ... a magnet."

I sighed dreamily. I knew that feeling all too well. "Maybe it'll work out."

"Maybe," Marina said, but she didn't sound like she believed it.

We turned the corner on Congress and MLK Jr. Boulevard to find Ash Talmadge waiting in front of Lulu's Chocolate Bar in shorts and a button-up. Marina waved at him.

"Ash!" she called.

He looked up at the sound of his name and smiled.

Marina gave him a big hug. "Good to see you."

"You too, Marina."

He shook hands with Daron and Tye. Daron shot me a look as if he knew exactly what I was thinking. That was the thing about Daron. He was so intuitive that nothing went over his head.

I pushed him inside. "We'll follow you in. Derek and Kasey grabbed a table already."

Marina grumbled, "Ugh. Do we have to hang out with her?"

"Unfortunately."

No one liked Derek's fiancée, Kasey. She was mate-

Wait for Always

rialistic and talking to her was like a read on how much money everyone spent each week. I just didn't care about it all and couldn't figure out why Derek didn't see it.

"Order me the chocolate chip cheesecake," I told Marina.

"Will do." She squeezed my hand and then followed the guys inside.

Anticipation tore through me. I'd been waiting all day for this moment. Ready for Ash to talk to me. I'd come up with a million scenarios, and though I'd downplayed it to Marina, I couldn't deny that at least half of them were us riding off into the sunset together.

"So, you wanted to talk to me?" I asked.

"Right. Yeah. You don't want to go inside and eat first?"

"Have you ever been told someone wants to talk to you and then walked away? It's been on my mind all day," I said with a laugh.

"Shit. Didn't think about that. It's not bad."

"Well, that's good," I said with a laugh.

For all of the possible things that had gone through my mind when he said he wanted to talk to me, not a single one of them prepared me for what he said.

"I got into an MBA program."

My mouth opened slightly, and confusion flittered across my face. "What? An MBA? What do you even need an MBA for?"

He shrugged. "I really don't since I'm working for my dad. But then again ... I'm working for my dad."

"Right," I said slowly. "Being your own boss is preferable, but you're not leaving Talmadge Properties?"

"No, I'm not. UGA has a program in Atlanta, and we have an Atlanta office.. I'm going to take classes on nights and weekends while working for the business from there."

My heart stopped. "Atlanta."

"Yeah. I start in August."

I was going to be sick. "You're moving to Atlanta next month? Does Derek know?"

"I still need to tell him. Well, I was going to tell you all together, but you sort of jumped the gun." He laughed and ran a hand through his hair. "So, I'll get my MBA and get to be out from under my dad."

"That's ... wow. Congratulations," I said, pushing myself into his arms.

He hugged me tight as the dreams I'd had burned to ash.

It was stupid. Again. So stupid. Why had I thought for a second that he was going to choose me? That didn't even make sense. I'd thought I'd gotten over so much of that feeling. I hadn't realized how ingrained it was in me until he gave me a tiny bit of hope and then shattered it like glass.

He didn't want to be with me. He'd helped me open my boutique, and now, he was getting the hell out of town. After telling me that Savannah was home and reeling me back in, he was leaving his own home.

"I'm excited. It'll be good to have a new opportunity like this."

"For sure," I said, pushing away my own feelings about the matter.

Ash and I were ancient history, and I needed to get that through my head. I just needed to be happy for my friend. So, I brought out a smile—a real one.

"Let's go tell Derek. Though he might hate you for leaving him behind."

Ash laughed, relief hitting his features when he saw that I wasn't mad. "Probably. Y'all will have to visit."

"Obviously," I told him.

I took his arm and drew him inside, ready to see my brother's reaction to Ash leaving. And knowing this was the nail in the coffin of our relationship that I'd tried to rise out of all afternoon.

13

SAVANNAH
DECEMBER 25, 2017

My dress was Christmas green, my lipstick was Christmas red, and everything was all right at our annual Christmas party. Dad had been having it before he and Kathy got married, and he'd had it every year since too. We all went to church for Christmas Eve Mass, Dad threw one giant party for all of his friends the night of Christmas. The only year we'd missed it was when Dad's work had taken us all to Paris for the holiday, when I was in college.

This year was like every other year. Except I had a date.

"I got you more champagne," Smith said with a smile solely for me.

He was handsome, just the way I liked them. He'd been a Holy Cross boy in high school, a few years older than me. He knew Derek well enough to fear him, but he'd grown out of that boyish fear, and he was here at my side now. His father worked in the pharmaceutical business, and his mom was a state senator after years as an attorney. Smith was following in both their footsteps with an interest in politics as he worked for his dad's company.

Dad liked him. Which made me feel things that I couldn't articulate. Kathy just squeezed my hand as they hit it off like best friends and planned golf trips together. That was what I was supposed to want. It wasn't supposed to make me suspicious of my choices.

Derek appeared in a tuxedo then and nodded his head to the side. I knew precisely what that meant. Every year since we'd been kids, we'd escape the stupid adult party to hang out in the library.

I grabbed Smith's hand. "Come on."

"What?" he asked, distracted. "You go ahead. I'm speaking with your father."

I opened my mouth to remind him that he was dating me and not my dad, but the words died on my lips. "Fine. We'll be in the library if you want to join."

His eyes softened at those words. "I'll be there in a minute."

I downed my champagne on the way and left it on a table to be scooped up. Derek would have the good stuff in the library anyway. I stepped inside and found Kasey lounging on a chaise next to one of her girlfriends. They were both smoking pot. The room reeked of it. All those poor books.

Derek handed me the bottle of scotch he'd filched from Dad's supply. "Where's Smith?"

"Talking to Dad," I grumbled before taking a drink straight from the bottle.

"Lovely."

"Tell me about it."

The door creaked open again, and I turned, hopeful that Smith had actually followed me. But the person who walked through made my heart skip in a completely different way.

"Ash!" I said in surprise.

He winked at me and shut the door carefully behind him. He was in a navy suit and tie with his dark peacoat still around his shoulders from the chill outside. Then, he held up two bottles of Dom that were old enough to make my head spin. "Sorry I'm late. Had to sneak these past my dad."

"What is with y'all and stealing from your parents? Don't you know you're adults?" Kasey sniped.

Derek shot her a look. "It's part of the fun, Kasey. It's how we've always done it."

"You turned thirty this year, Derek," she said, hopping off the chaise and walking toward Ash. "You should act like it."

Derek snorted. "Whatever. That's overrated."

Kasey snagged the second bottle from Ash and kissed him on the cheek. "Good to see you."

"Kasey," he said politely.

Ash had been the best man at their wedding. But I

Wait for Always

wasn't sure he liked Kasey any more than I did. His smile even faltered when he looked at her but only for a minute. He must have already been pretty drunk if he was this happy. I hadn't seen him like this in forever. Well, I hadn't seen much of him since he'd moved to Atlanta. Which had ended up being a good thing for my crush. Now, I was with Smith and Garrett before him. Working my way through every available hot Southern gentleman in the vicinity, was what Derek said. Whatever.

"Anyway," Derek said, brushing aside the fight with Kasey, like he always did, "you're lucky you brought a consolation present. You didn't make it to Mass last night."

Ash grinned like a fool. "Yeah, I got caught up."

"I know you were home, fucker," Derek said, popping the cork on the first bottle and taking a long sip. He passed it to me. "Damn, that's the shit."

I took my own sip. Smooth. "Where were you anyway?"

"I thought we could have a toast," Ash said. "Should I get some glasses?"

"Don't bother," Derek said. He was definitely drunk already. He collapsed back into a chair and reached for the scotch again. "There're enough bottles here that we can do it like this."

He offered Ash another bottle of whiskey, which he took with a shrug.

Then, there was a knock on the door. We all looked

around. Who would knock? The parents knew about our Christmas Day library festivities, but they didn't bother us.

Ash cracked the door open, hiding the booze as if it would stop the smell of pot drifting down the hallway. But it was Smith who smiled sheepishly.

"Hey," he said. "You're Ash Talmadge."

Ash arched an eyebrow at him. "Yeah?"

"He's with me," I said quickly.

Ash glanced over at me and then back to him. He held the door open a little wider. "All right."

"I'm Smith," he said, offering Ash his hand.

They shook, and for a second, I thought he was going to start chatting up *Ash* about business too. The man didn't seem to care about much else. But he walked over to me and put an arm around my waist. Everyone watched us as if we were a spectacle.

"So, a toast?" I said quickly.

"Right," Ash said, holding his bottle up.

"What are we toasting to?" Derek asked.

"Well, I have some news. Lila and I got back together."

I nearly dropped my bottle of champagne. I barely caught it by the neck, and Smith gave me a disapproving look. My jaw was already on the floor anyway.

Derek was drunk, but not stupid. His jaw dropped and then he jumped to his feet. "How did this happen?"

"We met at the fountain last night. She missed me. We're going to try it again."

Derek looked like he wanted to give him hell. And, *fuck*, I wanted it to be Derek to tell him that he was an idiot. Because what in the actual hell was he talking about? Not only had Lila cheated on him and left him a few years ago, but he'd also gotten into some huge fight at the church last year with her new boyfriend. It had been horribly embarrassing. I couldn't see why he'd ever want to see her again, let alone *get back together with her*.

But Derek didn't do or say any of that. He just laughed and held his bottle up to clink against Ash's. "Congrats, man. I know that's what you've wanted all year."

Ash grinned. "Thanks, man."

"To you and Lila."

Everyone raised their bottles and drank deeply from them. Smith held up his champagne and then headed over to Ash to give him proper congratulations. As if he had any fucking idea what all of this meant.

But I couldn't do it. I couldn't stand here and act like it was a good thing. This wasn't even about me and Ash. This was about him going willingly to his own death. I wouldn't be party to that.

I made some excuse. The words left my mouth, but I had no recollection of what I'd said. Then, I walked through the double doors that led from the library to the backyard beyond. It was too cold for anyone to be out here, and I hadn't grabbed a jacket, but I didn't care. Not in that moment. Not when my anger propelled me forward.

My dress was long-sleeved and knee-length, but I'd skipped tights, knowing I'd stay inside all evening. I was shivering almost immediately as I leaned against the railing that led down to the covered pool. But I wasn't ready to go back in. The library had been a sanctuary all those years. Now, Smith was waiting for me inside, and Ash had dropped a tragedy on our door. One that he was *happy* about. I just didn't understand. I didn't understand him at all. What hold did Lila Greer have over him?

I'd only been outside a few minutes when I heard footsteps approaching. I assumed it was Smith and turned to face him, prepared to tell him that we should go home. But it wasn't Smith.

It was Ash.

"Hey," he said, that smile faltering.

"Hey."

"You're freezing." He slid out of his peacoat and wrapped it around my shoulders. "What are you doing out here?"

"I don't know," I lied. "Did Derek send you after me?"

"No. I think he's trying to figure out your new boyfriend."

"Good luck to him. I still haven't figured him out yet."

Ash leaned next to me. "What's with you?"

I faced him, not able to hide my irritation. "What do you mean?"

"You seem pissed."

I clenched my jaw. "You should go back inside."

"I don't want to go back inside," he told me. "I want to know what's going on with you. You've been weird since I moved to Atlanta. We used to be friends …"

A laugh punched out of me. "Friends."

"What? Weren't we?"

"We were. We are," I corrected. "It's not that. Tell me, Ash, did you move to Atlanta to be near Lila?"

He opened his mouth and then closed it. "I mean … it wasn't the only reason."

I clenched my jaw and nodded. "That's what I thought."

"What does that have to do with any of this?"

"You're an idiot."

"*I'm* an idiot?" he asked in shock at my words. "What the hell, Mia?"

"Don't *Mia* me," I snapped at him.

"Is this about what happened in New York? That was so long ago."

"No. It has nothing to do with that. It has everything to do with why you came to New York to see me in the first place. Why you slept with me when you did visit."

He glanced behind him, as if expecting Derek to

hear that confession I'd kept behind my teeth for three years.

"He's not coming out here. He's drunk, Ash."

"Maybe you are too."

"I'm not. I'm just the only person who will tell you the truth."

His eyes narrowed. "What does that mean?"

"That you and Lila shouldn't have gotten back together. It's a horrible fucking idea, and you and I both know it."

Ash straightened at my words. "I don't know that. I don't know that at all."

"You two are awful together. She cheated on you," I spat at him. "You fought over her last Christmas. She didn't *choose* you, Ash. Why are you falling all over yourself for her? Why are you so obsessed with her?"

"You don't know her, Amelia. I love her."

I nearly gagged at those words. "If that's love, then I don't want it."

I turned to walk away from him, but he grabbed my arm and swung me back around.

"And what do you know about love? That guy in there, your boyfriend, do you love him? What about the last one? What about the one before that? Have you ever been in love?"

I yanked my arm out of his grasp. "Yes," I said hoarsely. "I was in love with one boy, and he used me for sex to get over his cheating ex-girlfriend."

Ash's mouth dropped open at my admission. At the

lie that I'd told him all those years ago after we hooked up. He'd never known the truth about how I really felt about him. About how my entire world revolved around his perfect, chiseled jaw and bright blue eyes and big, romantic heart. How one look from him could change my entire life.

And I hadn't wanted him to know. I'd wanted him to think that we'd had a good time and it hadn't mattered. But it was out in the open, and I regretted it with everything in my being. Now, he had all the power again.

"You didn't love me," he said as a defense.

"You don't get to tell me how I feel."

"Feel," he said softly. "Present tense."

"Felt," I corrected.

But it was a lie.

We both knew it was.

"Mia," he said softly, "I don't know what to say."

"Don't say anything."

I took off his peacoat and tossed it back to him. He caught it with one hand. There was so much pain in his eyes, and I hated being responsible for it. But now, all of my secrets were out in the world. He had every single one.

If I could go back in time and change anything, I would have kept at least that I loved him to myself. But I still would have told him the truth about Lila. He needed to hear it from someone. Even if it didn't make a difference.

14

SAVANNAH
JUNE 15, 2019

*D*erek pulled on the jacket to his suit. "How do I look?"

I shrugged. "Good."

"Good, Mia?" he asked. Derek turned in a circle with a smirk. "I look better than good."

"If you say so," I joked.

He always cut a sharp figure in a suit. He knew that.

"What are you wearing anyway? You can't go to the wedding like that."

I was sitting around in jean shorts and a pink crop top. My hair was in a messy bun on the top of my head. This absolutely was not wedding appropriate. "I know."

"Did you design something for it? You haven't said anything about it."

I shook my head. That was a definite no. "I'm not going."

Derek jerked his head away from the mirror, where he'd been adjusting his bow tie. "What are you talking about? It's Ash."

"Yep."

Ash Talmadge was marrying Lila Greer today at the church we'd all grown up in. It was the event of the season from what I'd heard. People coming in and out of the shop had all been discussing what to wear to it. The church was going to be packed full with some four hundred guests. But I wasn't going to be one of them.

"He's my best friend, and you've known him your entire life."

"Well aware, brother mine."

Derek crossed his arms over his broad chest. "Marley is a bridesmaid. It's not going to be fucking easy for me."

He and Marley were on the outs of course since he'd married Kasey.

"Okay," I said with an unconcerned shrug.

"And I know you've had a crush on Ash since you were a kid, but it's his wedding day."

"This has nothing to do with how I ever felt about him. I am *not* going to watch him marry Lila."

"And why not? Because you're jealous?"

"Fuck you," I spat.

Derek's eyebrows rose. We joked around a lot and cajoled each other. We were still siblings after all. But we were never actually mean. He'd touched on a nerve, and now, he knew it.

He sank down into the seat next to me. "What's this about?"

"Ash knows exactly how I feel about this thing with Lila."

"And what is that?"

"That he's an idiot for getting back together with someone who cheated on him," I said hotly. "That's not love."

Derek sighed. "Is this about Dad?"

I jumped out of my seat. My face hot as a brand. "No!"

"Mia," he said consolingly, "I'm not attacking you. Sit back down and talk to me about this. I know things with you and Dad have been shit for a long time. He cheated on Mom. She left because of him. He married Kathy."

"I know all of that," I said, suddenly feeling fragile. "And I love Kathy. I don't blame her."

"You blame him."

I turned away from him. I did. I *did* blame Dad for what had happened. He was the one with wedding vows. He was the one who had ruined our lives for a younger woman. "So?"

"And now, you're blaming Lila and punishing Ash for it."

"He's making a mistake," I told Derek.

"He's still your friend. Friends make mistakes, and sometimes, we have to stick by them, even when you think they're making a mistake," Derek said. "I don't want to go. There's no lost love between me and Delilah Greer." I winced at the sound of Lila's full name. "She hurt my friend. But he loves her, and so I'll stand by him, no matter what. You should too. Even if you're still mad at Dad."

I squeezed my eyes shut. "I *can't*, Derek. I can't."

"Why?"

I gulped and finally met his concerned eyes. "Because we slept together."

Derek's jaw dropped, and then he looked furious. "I'll kill him."

I grabbed his arm before he could do something stupid. "No, stop. Look, it was a long time ago."

"I don't care when it was!"

"Derek," I groaned. "It's his wedding day. You said you'd be there for him. You can't hurt him because of our ancient history."

"When?" he demanded.

"Remember when y'all came up to New York after he and Lila broke up?" Derek nodded. "It happened after you left."

"The fuck?" he growled.

"And that might have been fine ... if I hadn't told him I was in love with him when he told me he was getting back with Lila at Christmas."

Derek pushed a hand through his hair. "Fuck."

"Yeah. It was ... a mistake. I should have never said anything. But I can't take it back, and I won't stand there when he makes his mistake. Do you understand?"

He finally nodded. "Okay, Amelia. Okay. I wish you were coming, but ... I get it. I'll kick his ass *after* the wedding."

I snorted. "Fine. After though."

He ruffled my bun, and I jerked back.

"You know he never deserved you, right?"

I bit my lip. "Thanks, Derek."

He finished getting ready and then headed out to the wedding of the season.

I curled into a ball and turned on mindless television to try to silence my mind. But it was no luck. Ash was going to be married in a matter of hours, and then he'd be out of my reach forever.

Nothing was on TV. My email was empty. The internet was silent.

And I was going stir-crazy.

It was half past four o'clock. Ash should be married already. Pictures would start showing up on social media. I should be enjoying the silence and not waiting for the barrage of images that were surely going to break my heart.

I groaned in frustration. This was stupid. I should have just gone. Then, at least I'd know when it was over. I'd have seen it all firsthand instead of waiting with anticipation for it to cross my feed.

Then, my phone rang. Derek's number came up. That was weird.

I answered. "Hey. What's up?"

"Grab alcohol and meet me at my house."

"What?"

It sounded like he was driving. But why would he be driving? Shouldn't he be at the wedding?

"Hurry."

"Derek, what's going on? Aren't you at the wedding?"

Derek was silent for a few seconds, talking to someone else in the car. Then, he said, "I'll explain everything when you get here."

The line died. What the hell?

Well, fuck. I grabbed a few bottles of wine and two bottles of scotch I'd been saving for a special occasion, dropped them in a bag, and then got in my car. I parked out front of Derek's house. His BMW was parallel parked in front of his place. He'd done a shitty job with it. I'd never seen him park that poorly.

What in the fuck was going on?

I pulled into the spot behind him and jogged up to the front door. I wrenched it open without knocking and found Ash Talmadge pacing in the living room.

"Ash?" I said in confusion.

His head whipped up at the sound of my voice. He was still in his suit from the wedding. His bow tie was hanging loose around his neck. The top button undone. His face a mask of fury.

I nearly stepped back. But then Derek strode in with a bottle. He shot me a frantic look.

"Hey, Mia. What did you bring?"

I opened and closed my mouth. Then, I held up the bag I'd carried inside. "I have scotch." I glanced between them. "What is going on?"

"Just tell her," Ash spat.

Derek took the bag from me. "Lila left."

"She ... didn't show?"

"No," he said with a sigh.

"Cole interrupted," Ash spat. "And she left with him."

My stomach dropped. "No," I whispered. "That's ... oh my God."

Derek rummaged through my bag and poured out three glasses of the good scotch. It seemed fitting. I'd been saving it for something special. I supposed the worst day of Ash's life counted.

"Ash, I'm so sorry."

He waved his hand at me. "Don't lie to me."

I winced. "I'm not lying."

"You weren't even there," he accused.

"That's not her fault," Derek said, speaking up for me. "Is it?"

Ash glanced between us, and in that one look, he seemed to realize that I'd told Derek everything. "Ah, so you know."

Wait for Always

"Yeah, you should have told me, but we have more pressing concerns now," Derek said. "So, have a drink."

Ash drained it and then threw the crystal glass across the room, where it connected with the fireplace and shattered. I jumped at the violence of the action. Derek looked helpless. I felt just as helpless. I didn't know how to help Ash. Nothing could help him. Lila had left with someone else. The real and final end. She'd made her choice, and it hadn't been Ash after all.

He sank down onto the table and put his head into his hands. "I'll clean that up," he muttered.

"Don't worry about it," Derek said. He shot me a beseeching look and then headed into the kitchen to find something to sweep up the broken glass.

I didn't know how to handle this situation, but I couldn't leave him all alone when he was hurting. This was a magnitude more terrible than when he'd come to me in New York, broken. How would he recover from this?

Still, I stepped forward and sank into the couch in front of him. "Hey."

He lifted his head to meet my gaze. His eyes were red. "Are you going to tell me you told me so?"

"No," I said softly. "No, I'd never say that. I didn't want this for you."

"Didn't you?"

"Of course not. I never wanted you to be hurt, Ash. I wanted to be wrong about her. I wanted you two to live happily ever after. I might have had feelings for you, but that had nothing to do with me wanting you to be happy."

He nodded once. I wasn't sure he believed me. But as much as I disliked them together, I wouldn't have wished this on anyone. Definitely not someone like Ash with such a big, open heart. What was this going to do to him? Fuck.

"You're the only one who told me," he said, clasping his hands together in front of him, his elbows on his knees. "You're the only one who warned me."

"I'm the asshole, Ash. You didn't want to hear it."

"That doesn't make you wrong."

"I'm sorry," I repeated.

"Thanks for showing up ... even though you didn't have to."

"You're one of my best friends. If you'd told me to come to the wedding, I would have done that too."

"I didn't want you to be uncomfortable," he admitted.

Ah, that big heart of his.

"I'll always be here."

He nodded as tears came to his eyes. My heart broke all over again for him. He leaned forward and wrapped his arms around my middle. I held him like that as his pain ebbed and flowed. There was nothing sexual, none of my feelings attached to the moment. I wasn't here for him as I always had been before. I just wanted my friend to stop hurting. I wanted to help him get better. And I'd be here as long as he needed me.

15

CHARLESTON
PRESENT

The wind whipped through my hair as Ash turned off of Highway 17 toward Charleston. We'd made good time in his Range Rover. Truthfully, I was glad that I hadn't had to drive. I'd never gotten over my years in New York City. I hated driving. Anything longer than to work and Ash's and back was too much. Why didn't we have high-speed trains for all of this?

"Your hair is wild," Ash mused as the speeds lowered and we pulled into the city.

"It's always like this in Charleston. We were feral children."

He laughed. "Oh, I remember. You and Marina would run around, screaming like banshees."

I arched an eyebrow. "So, how is that different than now?"

"Guess we'll see when we get there."

He reached across the console and took my hand in his. I swooned all over again.

The last three weeks with Ash had been ... everything I'd ever wanted it to be. We had lunch almost every day during the week and spent all weekend together. Despite all of that time together, we were taking it slow. At least physically. I might have wanted to go faster and further, but I knew it wasn't a good idea. Not with our messed up history.

When I'd invited him to come to Charleston with me, he'd picked me up and swung me in a circle. As if that whole time, he'd been afraid I'd drive off into the sunset and never look back. It was hard to even consider that when the man of my literal dreams was pursuing me with single-minded determination.

Ash parked on the street in front of the house Marina had rented downtown. "I'll get the bags. You go say hi."

And then I was out of the SUV, dashing up the sidewalk and to my cousin's house. She opened the door before I got there, as if she'd been waiting for me all this time. She threw her arms around me.

"Mia!"

"Rina!"

She laughed. "It's been too long. I can't wait until you move here."

"Don't get ahead of yourself. I don't even have the proposal approved through the company."

"Whatever. You're brilliant. Your company is brilliant. You'll do great." She winked at me. "Now, let me see this hunk of a boyfriend."

Boyfriend.

The word sent a shiver through me. Ash Talmadge was my boyfriend.

Ash had a duffel thrown over his shoulder and my suitcase in one hand. He waved at Marina with the other. "Hey, Marina."

"Ash Talmadge, I have never seen you look so good."

He snorted. "Uh, thanks?"

"About time you realized my Amelia was perfect for you."

His eyes found mine. "I guess it was about time."

I flushed. "Shush," I said, pushing Marina. "Don't be embarrassing."

"Hey, I've always been rooting for y'all."

"That so?" Ash asked when he reached us.

"Duh. I was the one who told her to kiss you at Miss Georgia forever ago."

Ash glanced over at me. "I did not know that."

"Oh my God, let's not do this," I said, grabbing my suitcase.

Marina winked at Ash. "Let me show you where y'all are staying."

I hurried inside her house and found Melanie Bishop trotting down the stairs. "Mel!"

"Ahh," Melanie cried.

She flung herself into my arms. She'd been best

friends with Marina since Melanie's father had retired from the Air Force. Though they were a few years apart, they'd been on the dance team together, all while growing up together. Melanie had recently graduated a year early from UNC-Chapel Hill. She'd been there with her now ex-husband, who ruined everyone's fun. That guy still made me cringe.

"I screamed when Rina told me you were coming." Melanie twirled in a circle. "By the way, do you recognize it?"

"Is that my dress?" I asked in surprise.

"Yes! I ordered it online. I wanted to support you."

"I love it."

"You know how I've always had expensive taste," she said with a wink. "My sister says it like it's a bad thing, but how can she even talk?"

I laughed. Melanie's sister, Natalie, was married to Upper East Side royalty. I'd never crossed paths with her when I was with Camden, but it had shocked me to find out she'd married Penn Kensington. He was the person that Katherine and Harmony had fought over that one Fashion Week. He was hot, so good for her, but it wasn't a life that I would be able to handle.

"She has no room," I agreed. "I'll send you pieces of the summer collection if you want."

"I would love it. I adore everything you create."

Ash stepped inside, and I introduced him to Melanie. After we put our stuff in the guest bedroom, we came down to find Marina bouncing around.

Wait for Always

"I thought we'd go down to the docks," she suggested. "You ready to go?"

"Yeah. I was going to see Mom first."

"She's already there!" Marina said. "I checked with Dad."

Uncle Jacob was Mom's brother and the whole reason she'd moved to Charleston after the divorce. Having the support of her family here kept her sane. Or so she'd told me.

"All right. Let's go."

We left Ash's Range Rover and dropped into Marina's Jeep. The top was off, the windows rolled down, and the spring air blew through my hair. Ash slipped an arm across my shoulders in the backseat as we headed toward the water. I'd been so hesitant when he asked me out. It was hard not to worry that it would be like it always had been in the past. But as I leaned against his side, I felt for the first time like we were moving in the right direction.

Marina pulled up to the docks. We hopped out of her Jeep and headed toward Hartage Boating. Marina's family had had the boating business for generations. There were pictures inside of Uncle Jacob's house that showed him sitting on this dock with Mom at a young age. Alongside fuzzy black-and-white shots of their grandparents out on the dock. They'd been fishing, giving tours, and enjoying the waters for nearly as long as Charleston had been established.

Unfortunately, the family had hit hard times in the

last fifteen years, and what had once been a thriving business dwindled further every year. With all the money grabs by larger corporations, it was harder to make a decent living as a small business on the coast.

Uncle Jacob came out of the Hartage Boating building with a wide smile. He was as tan as his boys from days in the sun with sun-kissed brown hair and a trim physique. Aunt Lisa had passed from cancer after Marina went off to college, and still, it felt like a missing limb on the docks. Like she should have been right there at his side and not a ghost on the water.

"There're my girls," Uncle Jacob said.

Marina waved him off. "Hi, Daddy."

But I pushed forward into his arms. "Hey, Uncle Jacob."

"Good to see you, baby girl."

"You too. This is my boyfriend, Ash. You remember him?"

"I do remember him. The kid always running behind Derek."

Ash held his hand out. "That's me. Nice to see you again, sir."

"Well, let's get you inside. You know how to sail, right?"

"Yes, sir."

I rolled my eyes as Jacob dragged him along.

Marina looped arms with me. "You knew it was coming."

"Sure did."

Wait for Always

We followed them inside Hartage Boating, which was decorated with my mom's paintings of the business over the years. Some of them were from when she had been a kid, all the way up to her latest creations. Every single one was beautiful. I always said that I'd gotten my creativity from my mom.

"Hey, sweetheart," she said, appearing out of the back in paint-splattered overalls and her hair up in a bun.

"Hi, Mom."

It was still sometimes weird to see her like this. When she'd been with my dad, she'd been all prim and proper. And as her interior design profession had taken off, she'd dressed the part to get the kind of clientele who would pay for her expertise. But now, she had a thriving business, and so much of the work was passed to junior employees. So, she could be the painter by the ocean when she wanted to.

"Where's this boyfriend of yours?"

"Jacob took him out to the boats," I said with an eye roll. "As if you would expect anything else."

"True, true."

"And anyway, you've met Ash before."

"Of course," she said with a smile, wiping a smear of paint onto her overalls. "I remember the Talmadges well. He used to vacation with us here. But I've never met him as your boyfriend."

I laughed. "All right. Come meet him as my boyfriend."

A word I was still getting used to.

We followed the boys out the back of the shop and onto the docks, where the Hartage boats were lined up like ducks in a row. Even though Savannah was always home, Charleston was what summer was made of. The salty sea air, taking the boats out, finger food on the open water, tanning oil on the front deck, and Marina always at my side while the boys ran wild.

"Summer," I breathed.

My mom clapped my shoulder. "I know just what you mean."

Daron and Tye jumped off the boats they had been working on when they saw Ash heading their way. Mom and I followed them out to the boat, and I reintroduced them. Ash got along with everyone. He always had. He could charm his way into anything, even back into my good graces. Uncle Jacob started to make plans to take us out on the water and have a barbeque at his house later that night.

My eyes met Ash's, and he reached out, lacing his fingers through mine. This was how it always should have been. It was exactly right. And when he smiled at me, the entire world settled. It had taken us so long to get here, but maybe the time didn't matter. Maybe all that mattered was the here and now with Ash Talmadge at my side.

16

CHARLESTON
PRESENT

Nolan Holden shook my hand at the end of the meeting. "Thank you for meeting with me, Amelia. I like the proposal you laid out for including Ballentine in our brand-new luxury phase of Holden Holdings. I'm sure we'll have more information in the coming week."

"Thank you so much, Nolan."

I could feel sweat on the back of my tailored skirt suit. Nolan Holden was somehow both pleasant and downright frightening. He was nearly as tall as Derek with dark hair and eyes the color of summer storms. His jaw was square and razor smooth with disarming dimples when he chanced a smile.

I had no idea how Marina had ever had a thing with him. He seemed like the kind of guy who would eat the girl next door for lunch. Then again ... I'd dated Camden Percy. But he had chewed me up and spit me out like I didn't matter. I'd never gotten the truth out of Marina about what had really happened between them.

We said our respective platitudes, and then I hurried out of the shiny glass building on the water. Part of me felt like I was feeding myself to the sharks by working with the company buying up everything charming about the Southern coast. But if I wanted my business to thrive, I needed to be in with the latest trends, and that meant Holden Holdings. I had a much better chance at success if I had the backing of a big corporation.

When I stepped out of the business and into the sticky spring heat, Ash was leaning against his Range Rover. My apprehension dissipated when I found him waiting for me. His eyes caught mine, and he lit up.

"How'd it go?" he asked.

"I don't know. Good, I think."

He caught me around the middle and whirled me around, pinning me to the side of his car. "I bet better than good."

"We'll see, won't we?"

Then, he leaned forward and pressed his lips to mine, and I forgot all about my meeting. The anxiety about presenting in front of businessmen. The fear that maybe everything I'd worked for wasn't good enough. The desire to prove myself. It all melted away at his touch.

"That's not fair," I whispered.

He laughed. "What isn't?"

"How you can make me forget everything like that."

He arched an eyebrow and then kissed me again. "Like this?"

I squeaked as his tongue brushed against mine. "Yes," I gasped when he released me.

His fingers threaded up into my long hair. "I like that."

"Making me turn into a puddle at your feet?"

"Yes."

I choked on a laugh. "You're certainly sure of yourself."

"Is there a reason that I shouldn't be?"

His eyes were wide and unassuming, but I knew there was fear in that question buried deep. He'd had every reason to fear, as the only other relationship he'd really worked at had bitten him in the ass. I never wanted to make him feel that way. If we were in, we were all in.

"No," I told him truthfully. "You can always be sure of me."

His smile softened as he leaned forward for one more kiss. "Always have been."

He reluctantly released me, and we returned to Marina's. I changed out of my suit and into a different kind of suit—bright pink with strings on the side. Then, we went to the docks, where we'd promised my Hartage cousins that we'd go out with them on the water.

The sailboat was just large enough for the lot of us to be out. Jacob had closed the shop down for the day until they had sunset tours. But we had the whole day until then. Mom had packed a cooler full of sandwiches, snacks, and drinks. Marina and I took the bow of the sailboat and lathered ourselves with tanning oil, like it was old times. She was way ahead of me on her tan, and I was a little afraid that I'd burn, even with sunscreen.

"Remember when you used to drive the ice cream boat?" I said as I leaned back against one elbow.

"I still do sometimes," she told me. "On busy summer weekends, I can make nearly as much in tips as I do that week at work."

I snorted. "Ridiculous."

"You know rich guys like to tip big to pretty girls," Marina said with a wink. "Plus, I don't even make bad money at the center."

Marina worked as a small business advocate for a nonprofit. She'd majored in business at UNC, thinking she would run Hartage Boating with her family, but she'd been called to help others who were suffering under the weight of giant corporations. I felt a little bad that I was trying to work with Holden Holdings, considering her history with Nolan and her hatred for big businesses.

"Hey, you're not mad that I met with Nolan, are you?"

Marina rolled her eyes. "No. Of course not."

Wait for Always

"I know you have history."

"Ancient history," she amended.

"And it's your job to get more small businesses in the city."

"Yes. You'd still be a small business in the city."

"On his property."

Marina rolled over to face me. "There's a reason he's doing well, and it's not just because he has so much fucking money. I want you to succeed, Mia. Don't worry about my feelings."

"Okay," I said softly. I nudged her. "How did you ever date him? He was super intimidating."

"Says the girl who dated the literal owner of Percy Hotels."

"Fair," I said with a laugh.

I dropped the subject of Nolan Holden because it was clear that Marina had her own struggles with him.

Eventually, Mom walked to the bow of the boat to bring us sandwiches. She plopped down next to me, and Marina got up to grab us drinks.

"Perfect day on the water," she mused.

I nodded. "Yeah. I miss it here."

"But you're not going to move here," she said.

"What do you mean? If I get the property, I'm going to need to be here to run it."

She smiled at me and then brushed my hair back. "I love that about you, Amelia. I always have. The tenacity to get it done, no matter what. But you love that boy."

I wanted to protest, but I hardly could. We'd only been dating weeks, but I'd loved him for so much longer.

"You're not going to leave him behind, even two hours away."

"Why do you think I'm up here?" I asked in frustration. "I'm going to open a shop here."

"You still can, and you should," she encouraged me. "You can do anything you put your mind to, but this isn't where you belong. Trust me. I've known how you've felt about him since you were kids."

I glanced behind me to see Ash drinking a beer with my cousins and laughing with my uncle. It all felt so ... right. But he would never belong here. He would always belong to Savannah. Even when he'd gone away to Atlanta, there had already been a Talmadge Properties. It wasn't happening in Charleston.

"I don't want to lose him," I said. "It's taken us this long to get here."

"I know. I want you to know that I understand. Marina will understand too."

My stomach twisted. All of our plans about moving in together felt so long ago. But would I give it all up for a guy? I'd still have my shop. I could still open one in Charleston. I'd just run it from Savannah, right? Would I be doing this for a guy?

But it wasn't just any guy, was it? It was Ash Talmadge. He'd hurt me before, but as he'd said, we'd never really taken a shot at this. I couldn't give that up. Not when it was what I'd always wanted.

"And speaking of men in your life," my mom said with a shrewd smile, "have you spoken with your father recently?"

I groaned. Ash was one thing, but my dad too? All in one conversation?

"Amelia," she admonished, "he's still your dad."

"Kathy said the same thing. She wants me to come over. To try to make up with him, but we never even had a falling out. He should put in effort too."

"He should," my mom agreed. "We both know he's not that good with communication." I scoffed. That was an understatement. "But you're his little girl. I know he misses you."

"I shouldn't have to reach out to him if he won't reach out to me. I don't have to continue to deal with generational trauma that has nothing to do with me," I told her.

My dad was the only subject that got me this riled.

She smiled softly. "You're so stubborn, my Mia. Just like him."

"I'm not like him."

"You are in so many ways. Which is why you two are still butting heads when Derek has let it go. You caught his stubborn streak."

I didn't like that comparison one bit. Even if it was true.

"He knows where I live and where I work. He can make an effort."

My mom held her hands up. "Peace, Mia. I didn't mean to make you upset. I'm just being a mom."

"Why would you even want me to talk to him? You hate him!"

She shook her head. "I've never hated him, Amelia. We were just incompatible. We should have ended it before we did. It's a blessing that you don't remember the arguments."

But I did.

Derek and I both did. The fighting matches before Mom had finally up and left. It had been so much. And then I felt guilty that I was glad they'd divorced so it would stop. Then, when I'd found out Dad had cheated, that guilt had turned to fury that he had ruined our lives like this. I still blamed him. I didn't know how not to blame him.

"Just talk to him," Mom said, patting my knee as Marina came back with waters.

"Here you go," Marina said. She tossed one to me, and I caught it. Mom left at Marina's return. "What was that about?"

I took a long pull of my water. "Dad."

Marina wrinkled her nose. "Ugh."

"Yeah. Parents can't help but meddle."

We changed the subject to the cute new guy at her work, and I tried to forget about my mom's words. By the time we made it back to the dock, a little more sunburned than before, I wasn't sure how successful I'd been.

Ash wrapped an arm around my shoulders as we headed back to his Range Rover. "That was a great day."

"Besides my burn."

He laughed. "Yeah, besides that. Do you want to go out tonight?"

"What do you have in mind?"

"Well, Nolan texted me and invited me to a party."

"Party?" Marina asked excitedly as she came up behind us. "I love a good party. Who is throwing it?"

"Nolan," Ash said without having any knowledge of how that would make Marina react.

"Oh," she said. "Well, have fun."

"Come with us," I pleaded. "Bring Mel."

"No interest in Nolan Holden."

"We can dress you really sexy and make him wish he still had you."

Ash coughed. "Wait, you dated Nolan?"

"*Date* is not the right word," she grumbled.

"Come on, Rina. It's our last night in town."

Marina sighed. "Fine, but I'm not talking to him."

"Done."

Ash arched an eyebrow at me. "What's that all about?"

"Honestly, I have no idea." I bit my lip, second-guessing all of this now that it looked real. "It won't be weird that I'm doing business with him and showing up at his party?"

"Nah, he's an old friend. It'll be fine."

"If you say so."

Then, he kissed me again, and I forgot all about my concerns.

17

CHARLESTON

PRESENT

"Nope, nope, nope," Marina said, trying to turn around and head back to the car.

Ash and I both grabbed her to stop her from running away.

"Rina," I pleaded, "we're already here."

"And y'all have a great time. I'll come back later and pick you up even."

"What about this changes anything?" Ash asked.

We all glanced up at the enormous yacht in the harbor. It practically looked like a cruise ship. The thing had balconies and tiers and dancing women in thong bikinis hanging off the sides. It was ... elaborate, and I'd grown up with wealth. Ash had a yacht that was huge, but it didn't rival this thing.

"Doesn't it change everything?" Marina grumbled. "It's just so ... ostentatious."

That was probably true, but it was also awesome. And we were going to a party on it.

"You knew we were going on a yacht," Melanie said with wide, excited eyes. "Don't ruin this for us, Rina."

Marina groaned, "Not you too."

"As if I would ever pass up a mega-yacht party."

"I should have known," Marina said with a sigh.

"You can go home if you want," I told her. "But don't let him take away a good night from you. You don't owe him that."

That sparked something inside of her. She would never let anyone else win. Not when she could make them pay.

"Fine. Let's go on Nolan's stupid yacht."

Melanie linked arms with her, and they strode forward together. Ash shook his head as he wound our fingers together.

"She's something," he said.

"She really is. That's why I love her."

"You're still okay with this, right? Not worried about the business?"

I was actually. Though I wasn't sure how to tell him that. Not after my mom had gotten straight to the heart of the matter. How could I leave Ash to work? How could I leave work to be with Ash? It was a dilemma I wasn't sure how to fix. I had planned to leave Sasha in charge in Savannah while I took over in Charleston. She had been working with me from the beginning, and she could handle it. But what would happen if I wasn't in Charleston to get the business off of its feet?

My head felt dizzy with questions that I had no answers to.

So, I just smiled and nodded. "Let's go."

We were greeted with champagne flutes and escorted to the top deck, where a DJ had hits blasting through the speakers. The reason most of the women were in thong bikinis became evident by the massive pool in the center of the deck. There were nearly as many hunky, shirtless men in the pool, flirting with the women. It was complete with a champagne fountain, enormous buffet, and somehow ... a helicopter pad.

"This is insane," I said to Ash.

He grinned. "That's Nolan. Always over the top."

And then we found the man of the evening. Marina grabbed my other hand when she saw him. The world collapsed as he found us across the deck. Somehow, it was as if he only saw Marina. We'd dressed her in a skintight white dress that showed off her dark tan and curled her hair to supermodel waves. She looked like a vision, and Nolan was looking at her as if the very act of her stepping onto his yacht meant he owned her.

He approached us with two men and a woman at his side. His smile was straight feral. "You made it."

He shook hands with Ash.

"Couldn't exactly say no. Not in Charleston often enough to see you."

"Hey, Ash," one of the other guys said.

He looked a lot like Nolan. In fact, all of them looked similar.

"Rob," Ash said with a head nod. "This is my girlfriend, Amelia, her cousin Marina, and friend Melanie."

"Marina," Nolan said, snaking around the syllables of her name as if he were ready to constrict them.

Marina ground her teeth together and said nothing.

Melanie smiled warmly though. "Nice to finally meet you. Heard a lot about you."

Nolan arched an eyebrow. Then, he turned back to me. "These are my brothers, Rob and Ellis," Nolan said. "And this is Rob's girlfriend, Ever."

Ever pointed at Marina. "We've met before, right?"

Marina jerked her head away from Nolan. "Have we?" Then, Marina blinked. "Oh, wait, shit. Don't you work with Margie?"

Ever nodded. "Yes! I saw you at the company Christmas party."

"Margie, my mom?" I asked in confusion.

"Wait, are you Amelia *Ballentine*?" Ever asked.

I nodded slowly. "Uh, yeah?"

"I own the marketing firm that your mom uses for her company. My best friend is a senior interior designer there."

Whoa. Owns the marketing firm. Ever looked like she was barely in her mid-twenties. She must have been incredible to have her own company already.

"Small world," Ash said with a smile. As if he'd set all of this up.

Rob put a protective arm around Ever. She leaned into it, even as he dug his fingers into her side. As if she craved that harsh touch.

"Enjoy my party," Nolan said.

Nolan walking away was like letting the air out of a balloon. I glanced at Marina, who was still watching him like a prey tracking the predator in their midst. What a man.

"Come on. Let's get another drink," Ash said.

We fell into the fun of the party. Drinking the fancy cocktails from the bartenders, getting into the pool at one point, and dancing well into the evening. Even Marina seemed to calm down after Nolan disappeared. Like she was finally free without him. I made quick friends with Ever, who seemed like a hardworking girl. She had inexplicable bruises on her hips and thighs, made apparent when she shimmied out of her dress to get in the water. But she just winked at me when she saw me looking. Rob watched her like a hawk. I could only imagine what they did in the bedroom with bruises like that.

"Hey," Ash whispered against my ear. "Come with me."

"Where are we going?"

He didn't say anything. We just grabbed towels and our dry clothing, and I let him drag me out of the party. I'd only been inside to use the bathroom. The night was getting colder, and I'd been grateful for the heated pool. But it was too cold inside to be in a wet bathing suit.

Ash took the stairs down a level and then walked down an empty hallway. He seemed to find what he was looking for and pushed a door open. Inside was a bedroom. His lips crashed against mine.

"I've wanted you all night," he breathed in between kisses. "All day. You, in that bathing suit."

I giggled, drunk on Ash Talmadge.

While things had been progressing in the weeks since we'd first gone out, we hadn't yet crossed any lines. I wanted to cross all of them. I wanted to forget that the first time we'd ever done this had broken something in me. Write over that experience with new memories of us together. But I hadn't been ready.

As he dragged me into the darkened interior, all those walls came down. What was I waiting for anyway? If I was his, then I was his. I might get hurt, but I'd regret it more if I didn't try. If I didn't give him everything that was me. If I held back an ounce, then I'd never know the truth.

"Ash," I gasped as he kissed across my exposed collarbone.

He released me long enough to turn on a light attached to the side table. It suffused us in a soft yellow glow that highlighted my skin. Every bare inch of my skin against the hot pink of my bikini. Ash returned to me, dragging our lips together. He fiddled with the strings of my bikini.

"I've been thinking about pulling these all day," he confided.

"That would have been embarrassing."

"Not what I was thinking about," he teased.

"Oh? And what were you thinking about?"

"How about I show you?" It was a question to make sure I was okay with moving forward, but also a statement. That he was going to show me what he'd been wanting all this time.

The first tug came from my back. The laces that held down the triangle top were suddenly gone. The triangles doing nothing to hold my breasts in place any longer. His hands were there, pushing the material out of the way.

I gasped as he plucked at one of my nipples while he massaged the other breast. His smirk was so goddamn confident that I nearly fell to my feet in front of him right then and there. Why did I like it so much that he could take control of me like this? I had no idea. But I did want that. I wanted him to throw me on the bed and never stop until we were both so satisfied that we couldn't move.

The second tug dropped my bikini top to the ground. His mouth replaced his hand, and I arched against him. He swirled his tongue around my nipple before drawing it firmly in his mouth. When he nipped at it, I inhaled sharply, pleasure shooting straight through my body.

"Ash," I pleaded this time.

"Yes, Mia?"

But he didn't stop. Just switched to the next breast and took his time in bringing me closer and closer to the edge.

"I need ... I need you."

"Mmm," he groaned.

He tugged both strands of my bottoms at once, letting them fall to the ground. I gasped as he followed them to his knees, kissing down my stomach. He gently pushed me backward on the bed and spread my legs wide.

The first sweep of his tongue on my clit had me shaking with desire.

"Oh, Mia," he groaned as he slid a finger through my lips. "You're so wet for me."

"Yes," I gasped.

He thrust two fingers deep. "Are you going to come on my fingers?"

And I was. My eyes were clamped shut. My fingers fisted the comforter. He was moving with practiced, fingers out and deep back in while his tongue laved at my clit. There were so many sensations at once that I couldn't tell up from down.

"Tell me," he insisted.

"Yes," I moaned. "Yes, make me come, Ash."

He obliged with fervor, picking up his speed until

everything coalesced at once. I cried out as the first wave hit me and my walls contracted around his fingers.

"Fuck, fuck, fuck," I gasped.

He looked up at me, slowly withdrawing his fingers with a self-satisfied smile. "I've wanted to do that for a while."

"I ... should have let you." The words tumbled out of my mouth before I could stop them. I'd been the one hesitating this time. Too afraid to get hurt. But damn, hadn't we wasted enough time?

"I want to go at your speed, Mia. Not a second faster."

I reached for him, drawing his bare chest down against mine as I kissed him. I tasted my arousal on his lips. I could feel how turned on he was through the material on his sky-blue swim trunks.

I slipped a hand inside and withdrew his cock, stroking it up and down between us. His moan of pleasure was so satisfying that I didn't want to stop. I wanted more of him. I wanted all of him.

"Ash," I pleaded, "I'm ready."

He pulled back to look at me with surprise. "Are you sure?"

"Yes," I told him wholeheartedly.

"I'm not rushing you. I really wanted to get you off."

"I know," I said, a blush creeping up on my cheeks. "I want this. I want you."

He nodded. He really didn't need to be told a third time.

He stripped out of his swim trunks and produced a condom from the pile of dry clothes. I snatched it out of his hand, ripping the foil and fitting it down his cock. His eyes bored into mine the entire time as it slid down inch upon inch of him. Those eyes ... God, they were bursting with desire. He only saw me in that moment. Just me.

Then, he spread my legs wider and settled between my hips. Our eyes connected. He pressed a soft kiss to my mouth, and then he thrust home. I gasped into his mouth as he filled me completely. He slid out slowly and then bottomed out.

"Fuck," I sighed, meeting his eyes again.

"You feel so good," he groaned.

"So fucking good."

He started moving, and we worked a rhythm that felt as natural as breathing. Our bodies joined over and over as we panted into the dimly lit room. The whole time, I kept my eyes locked on his. My breath came out in uneven pants, and his back grew slick as I dug my nails into him. He picked up the pace, thrusting harder as we both abandoned everything for this moment.

"Close," I told him.

"Fuck," was all he said in agreement.

We both hit climax at the same time. My orgasm rocketing through me so hard that I literally saw stars on the back of my eyelids. Ash cried out into the room before dropping forward over me.

"Mia," he whispered as he kissed my shoulder.

"Hmm?"

"We're going to have to do that again."

I laughed but couldn't help agreeing. "Dear God, please."

Then, he pulled back to kiss me properly on the lips. He brushed a strand of my hair off my forehead. "I like this."

"This?"

"Us," he confirmed, looking into my eyes with all the earnestness in his romantic heart.. "I like us."

"I do too," I whispered.

And then he stood to head into the attached bathroom. I lay back, my body still processing the two intense orgasms and my mind reeling with the words he'd uttered. They shouldn't have been as groundbreaking as they were. He hadn't said he loved me or anything. But somehow, that look in his eyes had said enough.

Ash was all in. And so was I.

18

SAVANNAH
SEPTEMBER 21, 2019

Ash looked skeptically at the chocolate martini. "You're serious?"

I couldn't stop from laughing. I had to cover my mouth to hold it in.

Marley gave him a perfectly serious face. "Of course I'm serious. Amelia, take a picture."

"I'm not taking a picture," he said. Though he slurred half the words.

Ash had been drinking heavily since we'd gotten to Dub's this afternoon. It was his birthday. Lucky number thirty-two and just over three months since Lila had bailed on their wedding.

He'd really been doing nothing *but* drinking since that fateful afternoon. Derek and I were there for him as much as we could be, but it was nearly impossible. Especially since drinking meant he was fucking around with any pretty girl who walked past him. I hadn't seen him sober in months. This was the first time I'd seen him *alone* in at least a few weeks. Every time I ran into him, there was some dumb blonde on his arm.

I couldn't keep the disdain from my voice, but he seemed to not even hear it. He was so far gone after Lila that he just didn't process anything else. Which was why I was glad when Derek had proposed that we take him out for his birthday so he didn't do something stupid. Bringing Marley had been an interesting choice, considering she was Lila's best friend, but I knew Derek's endgame in this. He wanted Marley Nelson, and now that he and Kasey were divorced ... he had an opening. If he could kill two birds with one stone, why not?

Since I loved Marley and had hated Kasey, I wasn't opposed.

Just as long as it didn't trigger Ash into a deeper spiral.

No one said Lila's name. No one mentioned what had happened. Not a single word. The last time it had been discussed at all was that evening when I held him in my arms after he lost her. I wasn't sure drinking himself to death was better than that, but here we were.

"Smile, Ash," I said, pulling up my phone to take the pictures. "Pinkies out."

He laughed a real laugh and held his pinkie out as he lifted his chocolate martini next to Marley's. My heart fluttered at that sight. Derek and I exchanged a look. This was the closest I'd seen to the Ash we both knew and loved in a long time. Maybe he was finally coming out of it.

"There." I showed them the picture. "It's perfect."

Marley giggled and then took a long sip of her drink. She was also pretty wasted. Derek and I had stopped drinking a while ago. He wanted to make sure there was someone to take Marley and Ash home. I just didn't want to be that drunk around Ash. When my inhibitions were low, I knew where my heart lay. Even if, logically, I didn't want anything with Ash anymore, that didn't mean I *actually* didn't want anything with him anymore.

"We're adorable," Marley confirmed.

Ash snorted. "These are actually incredible."

"Told you!" Marley said, clinking her drink against his again.

I dug into the chocolate cheesecake while Marley and Derek ate the chocolate suspension cake, which was two layers of chocolate cake with a middle layer of strawberries and cream. All of it was incredible.

When we finished, Derek put an arm around a drunk Marley and helped her out of the restaurant. Something was *definitely* happening there.

"You ready to go?" I asked Ash. "I'll walk with you."

His eyes traveled down my body and back up. I flushed at that look.

"Sure," he said.

Wait for Always

"I'll get an Uber," Marley said, retrieving her phone and then promptly dropping it. She was wasted.

Derek picked up her phone and kept her upright. He shot me a look.

"I'll drive you," Derek told Marley.

I nodded. "Good idea. I'm going to walk Ash. It's not far."

"No way," Derek said instantly, looking at his drunk friend. "I'll drop you off too."

"I'm a hundred percent fine." I did a twirl to prove it to him. "I'll catch an Uber from his place."

"Text me when you're home."

I laughed. "Will do, *Dad*."

Derek shot Ash another alarmed look before relenting. He clearly wanted to get Marley home more than he wanted to watch whether or not Ash was going to do something stupid.

"Come on. Your place isn't far."

Ash slung an arm around my waist, and we walked through City Market. "I'm glad you're here."

"Me too. Even if UNC did lose."

Ash laughed. "Best part of my day."

I rolled my eyes at him. The Duke-UNC rivalry was legendary, and my entire family had gone to UNC. My mom and dad had met there. Derek had played basketball there. I had been born and raised a UNC fan while Ash had gone to Duke, just like his father before him. Even though it wasn't my alma mater, we still had the rivalry going. And UNC had had a devastating defeat in football earlier that evening. Which made Ash's birthday.

We chatted the rest of the way to Ash's house. I was glad that he lived so close to town. Though I could see how that was a problem for his drinking. It was probably why he knew all the bouncers and bartenders at every place we'd gone to tonight. If I hadn't seen a glimpse of the real Ash come out tonight, I would have been more worried.

This much drinking wasn't good under any circumstances. I had no idea how he was surviving at his job right now. I wanted to say something, but not on his birthday.

"Hey, Mia," he said as we reached the front door. "You should come in."

"I will help you inside."

He grinned devilishly as he took my hand and pulled me up the sidewalk to the front door. I shook my head at that look. He was literally drunk as shit and still flirting with me.

Ash fumbled with the key. Finally, I took it out of his hand and opened the door for him. He threw it wide and tugged me toward the entrance. I held my ground.

"Actually, I'm going to call an Uber and head home."

Ash gave me a charming look. "No. Come on. Just stay."

"I don't think that's a good idea."

Wait for Always

"Why not?" he asked, reaching for me again. He slipped an arm around my waist and pushed me against the doorframe.

"Ash," I whispered, my heart racing ahead of me. I didn't want this. Not like this. Not ever again. "You need to stop. You're drunk."

"Mia ..." He brushed my hair out of the way and smiled down at me. "I'm not that drunk."

I laughed and removed his hands from me. "You are. And I should head home."

He grabbed my hand before I could walk away. "Please stay. Come inside and have a drink with me."

"I can't," I said, my voice finally wavering.

If Ash had been asking this while sober, if things had been different, I didn't know if I would have been able to turn him down over and over again. Because even though this wasn't happening between us, it didn't mean that I didn't want it to. I just wanted him to be past all of this. I wanted him to be past Lila. But he wasn't, and until he was, it wasn't fair to me.

"You can." He brushed a kiss to my hand. I tugged it back, but then he stepped forward and ran his hand up into my hair. I tilted my head up to look at him. "I want this, Amelia. I know you want this too."

Then, he kissed me.

And oh, how I wanted that kiss to be real. For it to mean something. But it didn't. It just ... didn't.

"No," I said, pushing him backward a step.

He blinked at me in shock. "Amelia ... I ..."

"No," I repeated roughly. "No, you don't get to just kiss me whenever you want. I can't be used to forget her, Ash. You can use everyone else that way, but *not me*. Not again."

"Mia, I'm sorry," he said, his eyes losing the cloudiness of the alcohol as he realized he'd overstepped.

"Maybe you are, but you need to stop it, Ash. You need to stop drinking this much and fucking around this much. You need to see someone about what happened. You need *help*," I said, my voice breaking on the last word. "I'm your friend. I'll always be your friend, but I can't be more until you're better. Until you're ... over her."

He nodded once. His jaw clenched and his hands fisted. I could see it clear as day on his face. He wasn't ready for any of this. He'd just wanted to have fun, but I couldn't let him hurt me again like he had in New York. I wouldn't do it.

"Happy birthday, Ash," I said and then turned and walked away.

19

SAVANNAH
DECEMBER 25, 2020

Kathy was still dressed to the nines.

The annual Ballentine Christmas party had been canceled. It felt wrong not to celebrate the way we always had, but big parties weren't exactly done this year.

I was in a silky red dress that I'd designed but barely sold any of. I was drinking out of a flute of champagne, sitting on a velvet chair, as Kathy stared up at the Christmas tree. Christmas music filtered in through the sound system. Derek was still in Atlanta with Marley. They'd decided against driving down for the holiday. The holiday was sort of sad.

My dad appeared then in a tuxedo, and Kathy's face lit up as bright as the tree.

"Shall we?" he asked.

Then, he held his hand out, and she took it. He swept her up in his arms, and they moved around the room effortlessly. I could imagine the crowds around them, the laughter and entertainment. But this Christmas, it was just the three of us. I'd dumped my boyfriend a few weeks ago after he made fun of me for not wanting to take a real vacation this year. He was the third this year, and I couldn't bring myself to get back on dating apps. Why were all the men on them terrible?

"Come on, Amelia," my dad said, holding his hand out for me.

"I'm good."

He arched an eyebrow. "One dance for your old man?"

Eighteen-year-old Amelia would have laughed and let her daddy take her around the room. She hadn't quite despised him yet. But ... I just couldn't have it.

"Hard to be festive," I said as I came to my feet. "I'm going to the library."

My dad sighed and glanced down. "All right. Love you, honey."

"Love you too," I said as I retreated.

I caught Kathy's disapproving look, but she'd asked me to come over. We'd had dinner. I'd kept it together that long. I didn't want to dance around with him too. I should have gone home, but the library was tradition.

I snuck inside and was surprised to find the light already on. And not just that ... the double doors that led to the outside had been cracked open. Alarms went off in my head, and I reached for the handle again. But then I saw who had entered our home.

"Jesus Christ, Ash, you scared the shit out of me."

Ash stepped forward with a laugh. "Sorry. Sorry! I thought you'd already be here when I got in and I could tap on the glass to get your attention. Then, it was too cold. Do you remember last Christmas was, like, seventy? And this Christmas, it's only thirty-four."

I released all my anxiety and slumped back against the door. "Well, at least you're not an actual intruder."

"I thought I'd surprise you."

"Oh, I'm surprised," I said with a shaky laugh. "I thought you were going to kill me."

He laughed. "Someone has been staying up too long, watching true crime documentaries again."

"Guilty," I admitted with a laugh. "They're relaxing!"

"And look where that gets you. Jumping at shadows."

"Okay, but you were actually *there*. So, not just a shadow."

"Fine, fine," he said, producing a bottle of champagne and offering it to me. "I took this from my dad. You know it's tradition."

"I thought this was the year where we skipped all traditions."

He winked at me. "Not this one."

He popped open the bottle of champagne and

handed it to me. It was as cold as it was outside and tasted smooth all the way down.

"That's the good stuff."

I offered it back to him, and he took a long sip himself. The last year had been ... unprecedented. While it had been eighteen months since the wedding, we'd all been cooped up for a lot longer. I hadn't even seen much of Ash all year. Truthfully, I hadn't seen much of anyone.

He looked ... good. Okay, I was lying. He looked amazing. Like he'd been working out. His shoulders were broader in his suit. His waist tapered to perfection. The sharp cut of his jaw was somehow even more defined. Like he'd lost some weight ... or stopped drinking. Well, at least stopped drinking to excess constantly.

"You seem different," I admitted.

"Aren't we all?"

"True." I took another sip from the bottle.

"How's the shop?"

I shrugged. "Slow."

"It'll pick back up."

I nodded. I sure fucking hoped so. I couldn't keep living like this. Not with a small business in a tourist town with no tourists.

The silence stretched as we passed the bottle back and forth. But it was a comfortable silence. I didn't feel like I had to say anything here with Ash. Not as he perused my father's shelves while I lay back on the chaise. It was quiet and relaxed.

Ash moved away from the shelves and came to stand by my chaise. I passed him the bottle of champagne, which he took and set on a table.

He offered me his hand. "Dance with me."

I put my hand in his and let him pull me up. It felt like ages since we'd danced.

"Proper waltz or nothing, Mr. Talmadge."

He smiled at my behavior, and I saw the Ash I'd always known in that look. "As you wish."

The Christmas music was barely loud enough to reach the library, and we twirled around anyway, occasionally bumping into a desk or a chair. We just laughed through it. And for a moment, I felt like we were kids again. Just acting up and being silly together. No expectations. None of the years of problems that we'd dealt with.

"I missed you," Ash finally said when the dance ended.

"I missed you too."

"We should start to see more of each other."

"Is that allowed?" I teased.

"Lunch," he suggested.

"I'd like that."

It had been so long since things had felt normal. I liked that they were starting to feel that way with Ash again. He seemed to be on the up and up after what had happened. The world seemed to be going gradually back to how it used to be. Maybe it'd never be the same, but at least better than it had been.

Ash opened his mouth like he was going to say more, but loud noises from the living room stopped him. "What's that?"

"I have no idea," I said.

I pushed out of his arms and headed toward the door. I strode out into the hallway with Ash on my heels. The voices became clearer, and I broke into a smile.

"Surprise," Derek said with a laugh.

Kathy gasped and said something that didn't quite reach us. My dad's own booming welcome was heard loud and clear.

"I didn't think you were coming," Kathy said with even more excitement.

It was Marley who responded, "We hitched a ride with Lila and Cole. Decided to surprise her mom too."

Well, fuck. Lila and Cole. What terrible timing.

Ash skidded to a halt in the hallway just as I reached the entrance.

Marley caught sight of Ash, and color drained from her face.

"Ash," Derek said. "I didn't know you'd be here."

"We didn't know either," Kathy said. She raised an eyebrow at me. "Well, come on in. You're practically family."

I took a deep breath before turning back to look at Ash. Whatever our conversation had been in the library, all of his ease had disappeared. I hadn't exactly expected us to start dating or anything, but I'd thought maybe eighteen months was long enough that he'd be able to hear her name ... or Cole's name. But no ...

It was still too soon. He'd gone years and years without ever seeing Lila and still chosen her. What was eighteen months in the grand scheme of things?

I didn't expect him to want me. Not after everything. But I'd hoped for his sake that he'd let go.

"I'm actually going to head home. I just wanted to say merry Christmas," he said, forcing a smile.

"You don't have to leave," I said quickly.

"Stay," Derek encouraged. "It's the holiday."

Marley bit her lip and looked like she wanted to say more, but she didn't. She had been there at the very beginning of Lila and Ash's ill-fated relationship. She probably knew best that the whole thing was a lost cause.

"No, thank you, but I'm going to go. I'm sure my parents want to see me." He nodded at us.

"We're still on for lunch?" I asked.

Ash's gaze met mine, and there was a crack in the ice. Like I'd reached him somehow. He smiled at me and nodded. "Yeah. Lunch. I'll come by the store."

"Merry Christmas."

"Merry Christmas, Mia."

It wasn't until he was gone that we all blew out a breath.

Marley reached for me and pulled me into a hug. "I'm sorry. I had no idea he was here."

"Not your fault."

Derek crossed his arms. "He should be able to hear her name."

"He's still not over her," I announced.

"No," Marley said. "Do we think he ever will be?"

Derek shrugged. "Maybe when Lila and Cole get married."

"Is that happening soon?" I asked with wide eyes.

"I'm surprised it hasn't already happened," Marley said. "But I don't have any idea what Cole is planning."

"I'll have to tell Ash when that happens," Derek said with a grimace. "That will be a fun day."

"He'll be all right," Marley said.

But I had doubts. Ash had come a long way from the alcoholic that I'd known after the wedding, but I wasn't sure he'd ever be okay with Cole and Lila together. I'd hoped he'd be able to hear her name without disappearing. I'd hoped he'd moved on more than this. But I had just been kidding myself.

We could be friends, but nothing more. I wasn't going to ever get my hopes up again.

20

SAVANNAH
JUNE 19, 2021

"Wait, what?" I demanded of my brother over the phone.

"Cole proposed to Lila."

He'd called me while I was getting ready for Josie's party to discuss our upcoming sailing trip. I'd been expecting that we'd divvy up who was bringing what ... not *this*.

"Why are you telling me this? Does Ash know? We're all going out tonight, Derek! I don't keep secrets from him."

Over the last six months, things had changed with me and Ash. We weren't dating. I'd deny it to my grave, and Josie had basically asked me enough to make me feel like I might have to defend it that far. But we'd started to hang out all the time. We did lunch at least once a week. We went to the beach sometimes. We started going out with mutual friends. We'd gone to a party at the start of the summer, where I met my childhood star crush. Ash had kept his arm around me half the night. And still ... we weren't dating. Even if all signs pointed toward that.

Now, *this*?

Right when everything was going so well.

"I'm going to tell him after we sail up to Charleston."

Derek, Ash, Marina, and I were all going to get on Derek's boat and sail up the Intercoastal Waterway. It was our big planned trip. We'd been talking about it forever. How was I supposed to be with Ash for that much time and not have him know something was off?

I put my head in my hand. "Oh my God, you told me before we go sailing. We're all going to be on the boat for three days together. Why did you do this to me?"

Derek sighed. "Just keep it together. It'll be fine. I've known for weeks."

"Weeks?" I squeaked. "And you didn't tell him?"

"None of us even want him to know."

"None of us? Who knows?"

Derek groaned. "Well, me, Mars, Josie, and Maddox were all there when it happened."

"Josie knows? Jesus. We're going to her party tonight."

"I know. I know. Just don't say anything. What the fuck is he going to do if he finds out? Is he going to show up at their wedding?"

I froze at those words. I hadn't even gotten that far. I'd just been worried about him spiraling again. "Fuck."

"Exactly."

Fucking fuck.

"I hate you right now," I grumbled.

"But you won't say anything?"

"No."

And I hated agreeing with every fiber of my being.

I should have told Ash when he came to pick me and Marina up for the party. I was nervous, keeping things from him. I'd never done it before. I'd always been the only one who told him the truth. Fuck.

But I'd promised Derek. So, I reached for a pageant smile and got in his car and headed to the venue. It was the wrap party for Josie's *Academy* movie. Ash had reserved the space for her on River Street. It was surprising that they were getting along when I'd only ever seen some sort of general animosity between them.

Ash seemed happier than normal when we reached the party. He put an arm around my waist and walked onto the rooftop bar with me. I wasn't his date … but I wasn't *not* his date. The whole thing hadn't been confusing. Now, I wasn't entirely sure where we stood.

"You okay?" he asked.

"Fine."

"You seem jumpy."

I flashed him a smile. "Just happy for Josie and Maddox."

"They look happy," he agreed, seeing my friend and her boyfriend across the room.

"I'll invite them to sit with us."

"Sure. Let me grab drinks."

I sighed when he left, and Marina shot me a look.

"What is going on with y'all?"

"I won't burden you with that information."

Marina snorted. "Are you fucking yet?"

"Oh my God, Marina, no. We're not even together."

"Uh-huh. With his arm around you before he went to get your drink. Have you considered that you're dating Ash, but you just haven't admitted that you're dating him?"

Yes.

On multiple occasions.

But it was like approaching a butterfly. As soon as I got too close, it flew away. I didn't want to make things worse. We were friends. We weren't dating. Because I'd said I wouldn't date him unless he was over Lila. He might look at me like I was his entire world, but what did that mean in the face of multiple rejections?

Marina rolled her eyes. "Come on. Let's get our seats."

We invited Josie and Maddox to sit with us and made small talk until we heard a booming voice say, "Did someone say Ash Talmadge?"

I turned around in surprise to see a gorgeous man

stride forward and shake hands with Ash. He was tall with a navy-blue suit.

"Nolan!" Ash said in shock. "Fuck, man, what are you doing here?"

"Holden Holdings was part of the team to help with the movie. The director sent us an invitation to the party, and since I was already in town on business, I thought I'd swing by. Didn't think you'd be here."

"It's my building," Ash said with a laugh.

"Should have known."

I cleared my throat. "Introductions perhaps?"

Ash's eyes found mine, and the light in them was so bright. "Right. Yeah, sure. This is Nolan Holden. We went to Duke together. His family runs Holden Holdings, originally based out of Williamsburg."

Ash and Nolan went back and forth like old friends who hadn't seen each other in ages. It was kind of adorable. Except I was too aware of Marina shrinking next to me. I glanced at her in confusion, but she had all but disappeared behind me, as if she didn't want Nolan to see her.

I knew she'd dated a guy named Nolan. She'd told me he was a dick. But it couldn't be *this* Nolan, could it?

Nolan said something suggestive to Josie about her movie-star status, and Marina gagged. I smothered a laugh as Nolan's face snapped to her. The look was pure predator. It made me shiver.

"Marina," he said her name like stretching taffy.

"Nolan." Her response was all but feral as she came out from behind me to glare at him.

"What a surprise."

There was something between them here. Something that, at the first spark, would burst like a bonfire.

"I'm sure it is," Marina said.

I shot her a look. This *had* to be her Nolan, but Marina shook her head to tell me to stay out of it.

"It's been a while. Miss me?"

If looks could cut, Marina's would have gone for jugular. "That isn't the word I'd use."

Nolan just smiled wider.

I saw the moment when that look obliterated her anger.

She looked away from Nolan, backing down from the fight, then said, "If you'll excuse me."

"Marina, wait." I ignored the questioning looks and followed my cousin. "Marina." I grabbed her arm, yanking her to a stop. "Talk to me."

Marina clenched her jaw. "I ... I can't."

"Rina, it's *me*. You can talk to me about anything. Is that ... your Nolan?"

She nodded.

"What did he *do* to you? I've never seen you get this worked up about a guy before."

"Look, I wasn't expecting him here. I'm going to go home."

"Are you serious? Come on. Don't let Nolan drive you out."

Wait for Always

She shuddered. "I'm sorry. I want to stay for you, Mia, but I hate him. I just ... *hate* him."

I could see there was so much more than what she was saying. She didn't just hate him. She loved him too. She had to or else he wouldn't have been able to get under her skin like this. I knew that feeling all too well.

"All right. Here's my key." I pulled it out of my purse. "Text me when you get home?"

She nodded before pulling me into a hug. "Love you."

"Love you too."

I watched her walk away with a heavy sigh. So much for an uneventful night. Josie was onstage with her costar, talking about the movie, as I headed toward the railing of the rooftop bar. Ash came up behind me and wrapped his arms around my waist.

"Marina okay?"

I wanted to lean back into him. This had gone far enough. We needed to have it out as to what this *was*. I needed to know. I couldn't keep tiptoeing.

"She went home. Not sure what that was all about."

"Sounds like Nolan to me," he said. "I'm going to talk to him some more. Want me to get you a drink when I come back?"

"Yes, please."

He withdrew, and I shivered at the loss of contact. His smile was bright as he headed back to Nolan. There was practically a skip in his step. Fuck, I was in love with him.

I leaned far out against the railing, letting the summer air blow through my hair as I gazed out across the river. This was going to be such a mess.

A few minutes later, Josie stood at my side. "Are you trying to escape too?"

I managed a laugh. "Nah. Ash went to get drinks."

Josie asked about Marina, but I didn't even know what to say about that. Marina was usually so forthright. It wasn't something that I could figure out just yet. Especially when I was already trying to figure out what the hell to do about Ash.

I hung my head. "Can I talk to you about something else too?"

"Oh boy," Josie said.

"You can probably guess, but, uh, Lila?"

"Yeah."

"I don't talk about her or ask about her, but Derek called to discuss the trip, and he …"

"Yeah?"

"Ash doesn't know?"

"No."

"And you agreed to tell him after we get back?"

"Derek said he would," Josie said.

"I wish he'd never told me," I spat. "I feel real sick about knowing and not telling Ash. I don't even know Lila. She was two years ahead of me at St. Catherine's. We didn't really interact. But how do you think he'll react when he finds out?"

"That … I don't know."

"Do you think he'll ... try to stop the wedding?" I couldn't keep the panic from my voice. I felt young and stupid. I'd told myself I wouldn't fall for him until he was over her, and here I was all over again ... fucked in the head about it.

Josie's hand covered mine. "You're only hurting yourself, asking yourself these what-ifs."

"I know, but fuck," I growled, pushing away from the railing, "the bad timing. Did Cole really have to propose to Lila right now?"

A glass shattered behind us.

I whipped around to find Ash Talmadge. My hand flew to my mouth as I realized what he'd just heard me say. He'd been bringing me a drink, and it had slipped out of his hand to shatter at his feet. Glass covered the stone floor, and alcohol soaked his suit pants.

It was worse, looking into his furious eyes and pale face. Those blue eyes locked on mine. I felt suddenly sick to my stomach. This wasn't how it was supposed to happen. This wasn't how he was supposed to find out.

"What?" Ash asked, hard and flat.

"Ash," I gasped.

"Cole ... proposed to Lila."

"Yes," Josie said, stepping in for me.

"You knew?" he said, his eyes only for me.

"Yes, but ..."

"Did Derek know?"

I gaped at him. "He ..."

"Of course he did. Of course he fucking did."

"Ash …"

"Everyone knew," he finished.

I stepped forward, one hand extended to touch his sleeve, but he reacted immediately. His body shuddered as he flinched away from me and stepped backward. I stopped moving. Stood there, frozen in place, as Ash looked at me like I was the enemy. And I didn't know what to do or what to say. Not with that anger radiating off of him.

"Hey, what's going on over here?" Maddox asked as he appeared before us.

"I'm … going to go," Ash said with a head shake.

Maddox watched him walk away in confusion. "What just happened?"

"He found out about Lila," Josie said.

"Fuck."

"I should go after him," I choked out.

"No," Maddox and Josie said together.

Josie and Maddox made plans to help Ash, but I was still stuck. Right where he'd left me.

They were still talking as I muttered, "I didn't mean for that to happen." And I continued over their objections, "I shouldn't have hidden it from him." Josie tried to placate me, but I couldn't hear her. "Fuck. Fuck everything. Fuck this timing. I just thought we were …" I trailed off and swiped tears from my eyes. "I guess it doesn't matter. I'm … going to get someone to clean this up."

I disappeared before Josie could say anything else

that she thought would help me. I found someone to sweep up the glass and then sank down into a seat at the periphery of the party.

I'd told Ash all those months earlier that I wouldn't date him unless he was over Lila. And for so long, he'd given me every indication that I was the only person he was interested in. Two years almost to the day when Lila had walked out on their wedding, and I'd thought he was over her.

Had I just been wasting my time? Was I doing exactly what I'd said I'd never do?

Waiting for always.

Something sparked in my chest at that. Something *angry*. Something *furious*.

This was *bullshit*. All of it was bullshit.

I shouldn't have waited for Ash. He shouldn't have been acting like we were dating and stringing me along while he was waiting for Lila to take him back. The engagement was a wake-up call. Not for him, but for me. I didn't deserve this. I didn't deserve his anger. I didn't deserve to be kept in the wings, and I wouldn't any longer.

Maybe he should have some time to deal with learning about Lila and Cole, but I wasn't going to wait another day to have this out. It was now or never. Even if it meant never.

I headed out of the party without saying good-bye to anyone. Luckily, Ash's house was only a few blocks from here. I didn't even need to Uber to get there. My house was much farther, but I wasn't going there. Not yet.

The lights were on when I stepped up to the mansion Ash owned downtown. That was a good sign. I'd gotten halfway here and worried that he'd gone to a bar. But he was predictable at least in that he'd want to start drinking at home.

I rang the doorbell and waited for the door to open. When it didn't, I ground my teeth together and twisted the knob. It was unlocked, and I walked inside, uninvited.

"Ash?"

He didn't say anything, but I heard the sound of a chair scraping against the hardwood, and then his figure appeared in the hallway.

He held a crystal glass of some amber liquid. "What are you doing here?"

"We need to talk."

"No, I don't think we do," Ash said. Then, he turned and headed back into the living room.

"That's unfortunate for you because I'm the one who is here." I followed him into the living room. "And I say it's time to finally have this out. What have we been doing, Ash?"

He looked up at me with a raised eyebrow. "What do you mean?"

"You know what I mean."

"I don't want to deal with this right now."

"Why? Because Lila's getting married?"

He winced. "To Cole."

"Yes. The person she walked out of your wedding with. What did you think was going to happen? Did you think they wouldn't get married? Shit, I'm surprised it hasn't already happened."

Ash's eyes were molten lava when he looked up at me. We'd skirted around her name for ages. Been careful with his feelings, but enough was enough.

"Stop."

"No," I shot back. "Just *talk* to me."

"There's nothing to talk about."

"So, this ... this was just to pass the time?" I demanded.

"What do you want me to say?"

"I want you to tell me the truth. We've been tiptoeing around this. But everyone else already thinks we're dating, Ash. I've been giving you all the space you need. But I can't keep doing this if you still love her ... if you're still waiting for her."

His eyes were solemn as he assessed me. "The truth?"

"Yes. Stop wasting my time."

"I'm not wasting your time."

"Do you still love her?"

"I'll never stop loving her."

The words were a punch to my gut. Even though I'd been expecting them. "So, what? You're going to go to *their* wedding? Object like he did at yours? Try to win her back after she tossed you aside with such ease?"

He turned his face away from me, but I could see that he'd already been thinking about it. That he'd been plotting how to ruin the day.

"Lila picked Cole. She didn't choose you. If you show up at that wedding, you're only going to be hurting her. The person you claim to love."

"And don't they deserve it after what they did to me?"

"Deserve it?" I gasped in shock. "Were they terrible to you? Yes. Does anyone deserve to have their wedding day destroyed? No. If you love her, you wouldn't even be contemplating this. You'd want her to be happy. Because I bet you anything that she wants you to be happy, and you're not. You haven't been in two years."

Ash ran a hand down his face. "Amelia..."

"I thought you'd realized what you had," I spat at him. Tears came to my eyes, and I tried to wipe them aside. "I thought you were ready to move on."

"I couldn't lie to you."

I took a step backward. "As if that's kindness."

"Amelia, wait..."

But I shook my head. I had been the fool. Again. When I'd said that I wouldn't be.

"You do whatever you want, Ash. But know that if you go to that wedding, you will never see me again. *Ever*. It will be as if I never existed."

I didn't wait to hear what he was going to say or to see his expression. I didn't wait for any of it. I turned on my heel and walked out of his house. I'd been broken by Ash before. But this felt like the last time to me. I was going to start dating other people. I was going to find someone who cared about me as much as I'd always cared about Ash. I deserved that after all. I deserved so much more than that.

PART III

21

SAVANNAH
PRESENT

Josie turned in a slow circle. The wedding dress I'd designed for her hugged her curves and gave her an elegant appearance. It was her third wedding, third dress, third groom. And yet this was the only one that mattered.

"What do you think?" I asked.

Our eyes met in the floor-length mirror.

"It's perfect."

"We'll need to make some alterations now that I have the body done." I pointed out a few places that I wanted to take in and how much length I wanted to take off the bottom. "Here, here, and here."

"Perfect. We have plenty of time. The wedding isn't until June."

"Yep. Let me take some measurements. You're not going to lose any more weight, right?"

"Not with the way I'm cooking for Maddox." She

laughed. "I've been re-creating all of Gran's old recipes. Half of them use actual lard."

I giggled. "I bet they're delicious."

"I'll start bringing you the leftover pie."

"Leftover pie doesn't sound real."

Josie smirked. "Maddox agrees with you, but my hips don't."

"You're ridiculous. You're already small. Don't worry about it. Just be happy."

"Like you and Ash?"

I rolled my eyes at her. "Here it comes."

"I'm just saying ... I want the scoop."

"I know what you want."

Josie looked down at me as I pinned up a section of her bust. "The wedding is this weekend."

"I'm aware."

Lila and Cole would be tying the knot in Athens, Georgia, where they'd met in college, on Saturday afternoon. Derek had told me, like I needed to know ... like I even cared. I didn't know if Ash knew all the details, but I had to assume that he did.

"Well, is he ..."

I looked up at her. "Going to be there? No."

"You've talked about it?"

"Also no," I admitted.

"Amelia!"

"I told him last year that if he went to the wedding, he'd never see me again. That it would be like I never existed. I don't think he's stupid enough to do that. Not when we're actually dating."

Josie gave me a skeptical look. "For Lila?"

"Why don't you let me worry about Ash, huh?"

"Okay, okay," she said, raising her hands in surrender. "If you say so."

I bit the inside of my cheek to keep myself from saying anything more. I should have had this conversation with Ash already. That my words still held. That he'd never see me again if he went. But he'd admitted that he knew they were toxic and that they'd already had their chance. That was real progress for him. I didn't think he was going to destroy it all for Lila's wedding.

But ... I probably should make sure of that.

Damn it, Josie.

The minute I was out of work, I drove straight to Ash's instead of my own place. I'd been spending a lot of nights there since it was so much closer to Ballentine. But I definitely was not looking forward to this conversation.

I skipped up the front sidewalk and opened the door. "Ash?"

"In here, Mia," Ash called.

But I heard a second voice in the room, and my brow furrowed. "Derek?"

My brother stood in the living room. "Hey, sis."

"What are you doing here? It's a weekday."

"Yeah. I thought I'd drive down and see y'all."

I gave him a skeptical look. "Really?"

"Yeah. Do you want to go out with us?"

Ash walked across the room and pulled me into a hug. He dropped his lips down onto mine. "Hey, beautiful."

"Oh God, are you already drunk?"

Ash laughed. "We might have had a few."

Derek made a gagging noise. "Can you not while you're around me?"

"Fuck off," I muttered. "I already told you that we're dating."

"Yeah, but you're my sister."

I rolled my eyes. "You're such a hypocrite. You and Marley are all over each other around me."

"And?"

"At least he didn't threaten to punch me," Ash interjected.

"I'd kick his ass if he laid a finger on you," I snapped. "Don't come in here with your bullshit misogyny, Derek Ballentine. You don't get to have an opinion about my love life."

"He's my best friend," Derek said as if that explained it all.

"So, he's good enough for *you* to hang out with, but not *me* to date?"

"Yeah," Derek said with a laugh. "That's kind of the point."

Ash pulled me back from smacking my brother. "He's joking, Mia. He doesn't give a shit. He's happy for us. He's just trying to rile you up."

"And it worked," Derek said with a laugh. "Come on. Where should we go out?"

"I have work in the morning," I groaned.

"Call out."

"I *own* the business!"

"All the more reason," Derek said with a smirk.

I shook my head. "Fine. Let's go. I need to change."

I headed upstairs and found the stash of clothes that I'd left in Ash's closet. I pulled on a blue dress, applied some lipstick, and was ready to come downstairs when Ash appeared in the bathroom.

"Hey," I said with a smile.

"Sorry about Derek. I was going to text you."

"I don't really care. I miss him being here all the time."

"So do I," Ash agreed. "But we both know why he's here."

I arched an eyebrow. Were we finally going to have this conversation?

When I said nothing, Ash kept his eyes focused on me and said, "Because Lila's wedding is this weekend."

"Right."

"He's trying to figure out where my mental state is."

"And where is it?" I asked softly.

He pulled me into him. "Right here with you."

"You sure?"

"More than sure." He pressed a kiss to my lips. "I didn't forget what you said. That I'd never see you again. I wouldn't jeopardize us."

"And what if I hadn't said that?" I forced out.

His face softened at the words. "I'm here with you. Just you."

"You're sure?"

"I'm sure," he confirmed. "I don't need threats to stay with you. This is where I want to be."

The tension left my shoulders at those words. I pressed my lips to his, and his hands skimmed over my waist before circling around to my ass and pulling me into him. I would have given in to him right then if my brother wasn't waiting for us downstairs.

We broke away with a gasp. Pupils blasted out and breathing rough. He smirked down at me.

"Later," he teased.

"You'd better."

The wedding was still a few days away. I'd be lying if I said I wasn't still concerned, but I felt better than I ever had about it happening. This weekend, Lila would get married, and Ash Talmadge would still be mine.

22

SAVANNAH
PRESENT

The first Saturday morning in May dawned bright and beautiful. Ash was missing from bed, but that wasn't unusual. He was a morning person. Always up with the dawn, working out in the gym he had in the basement. He lifted weights and ran a few miles before I was even out of bed most days.

But today was different.

Today was Lila's wedding.

Nerves crept in at his absence. He wouldn't leave me here alone and drive into Athens, right?

I felt bad, even considering it, but it was hard not to think of all the other idiotic things Ash had done in the name of love. I wanted to say that the hold she had on him had snapped in the last year. That he was finally, officially over her. As much as he claimed that he was. On the other hand ... obsession was rarely logical.

"Ash?" I called as I threw on a silk robe and tiptoed out of the room.

I took the stairs in a hurry and glanced around futilely. The kitchen was dark. The living room looked untouched from last night. Even the glasses we'd left out were still there.

"Ash?" My voice was more frantic now.

I pulled open the basement door and rushed downstairs. The room was as empty as the first floor. No one was here.

Panic set in. I looked in the garage and saw his car was gone.

"Oh God," I gasped. "Oh God, oh God, oh my fucking God."

I raced upstairs, taking them two at a time in my haste. I nearly tripped on the top step. I threw my robe off and tossed it on the bed before scrambling into the first thing I saw—a pair of old cheerleading shorts and a tank top. I grabbed my purse and phone, which had zero missed calls or messages, and bolted downstairs.

I just made it to the last step, breathless and mildly terrified, when the front door opened. Ash walked inside, carrying a brown cardboard box of pastries and a holder with two coffees in it.

"Morning. You're up early," he said with a smile.

I could barely catch my breath at the sight of him. I closed the distance and threw my arms around him. "You're here."

"Uh, yeah."

Wait for Always

"I ... I woke up, and you were gone."

"I got coffee," he offered helpfully as I retreated.

He set the box of pastries from my favorite pastry shop, Back in the Day Bakery, and coffee on the kitchen counter.

"I see that." I threw my purse and phone down next to the coffee and flopped into a seat. My heart rate was slowly coming back down as the adrenaline left my body.

"You okay?" he asked, pressing a kiss to my lips before taking his own seat.

"We should go away today."

He arched an eyebrow. "Go where?"

"I don't know. Anywhere," I said quickly. "Let's take the yacht out."

His confusion disappeared as he realized what I was doing. He sighed and looked down at his coffee, steam billowing up from the lid. "I'm fine, Mia."

"I just want to do something," I said, reaching for his hand.

"I know what you're doing. We can stay here. You don't have to worry."

"I'm not worried."

He arched an eyebrow at me. "Your frantic run down the stairs and look of abject terror on your face were for no reason then, huh?"

I winced and looked down. "No. But when I woke up and you were gone ..."

"You thought I'd left...that I was going to the wedding."

"I'm sorry. You said you weren't going to go."

"No," he said, tilting my chin up to meet his gaze. "*I'm* sorry. You've done nothing but expect behavior I've shown you time and time again. I always went back to her. I made you wary of that. If I could go back and change it, I would. I'd fix how I treated you through so much of this. But I'm not leaving. I'm not repeating those mistakes."

"It's just ... hard to see that as true after everything."

"Yeah," he said with a sigh. "I won't lie and say I didn't think about it. Not because I still want to be with her. I didn't want them to end up together. Which I know how that sounds."

"Considering what happened at your wedding, it's reasonable, Ash."

"Yeah, but you were right last year. If I loved her like I said I did, then I should want her to be happy. And I do. I just don't want her to be happy with him."

I laughed. "That seems like a long way from the place you were in last year."

He took my hand in his. "So much of that is because of you."

"Nah. I was there all along. You finally came to your senses."

"Maybe I did."

"So, can we go away?" I asked gently.

"We can. But we're not running. Today is for us."

Wait for Always

"Okay," I agreed as he brought his lips to mine.

We ate the pastries and coffee. All the adrenaline had left my body, and in its place was relief. I hadn't realized how much fear I'd been holding, even as I told everyone else that it would be fine. Inside, I'd been slowly waiting for the end.

But this wasn't the end.

This was just the beginning.

Ash and I put on our bathing suits, packed a change of clothes, and headed out to the Savannah Yacht Club. While his boat was nowhere near as ostentatious as Nolan Holden's, it was still plenty impressive. He must have made some calls while we were getting ready because staff and crew were already waiting for us when we arrived. They took our bags, offered us drinks, and let us know that we'd be leaving within the hour.

We spent the day on the water, far from our phones and the reality of what our friends were doing that day. Maybe Ash didn't need to escape, but he seemed happier for the opportunity. It was just us in the sun and heated pool and even a very chilly drop into the Atlantic.

The sun was setting on the horizon as the yacht headed back into the dock. I snuggled into Ash's side in the hot tub as we watched the reds, pinks, and yellows burst across the ocean.

"This was a perfect day," he told me.

"It was."

"Thank you for suggesting it."

"Well, I had ulterior motives."

He laughed. "True. It did help me forget what the day was."

"Just made me realize that I want this to be my life."

His eyes slid to mine. "Oh yeah?"

I flushed as I realized how the words could be construed. "I just mean ... I want to be with you."

"That's not what you said," he teased. He wrapped an arm around my middle and pulled me into his lap. My legs straddled his hips. "You said you want this to be your life."

"You know how I feel about you. How I've always felt about you."

"Yes, but this already is your life, my Mia."

I leaned forward against him, letting our wet skin meet. "I suppose it is, but I might be moving to Charleston. Things will be more complicated."

"That's not going to change this."

"How do you know?"

He pulled me tighter against him, brushing his lips to mine. "Because I love you."

My heart stopped beating. Everything froze in place. I couldn't move or breathe or think. There was nothing but those words ringing in my ears.

"You ... love me?"

"I thought it was obvious." His hand slid up into my wet hair. "Of course I love you."

"I love you too," I whispered.

And the words felt truer than they ever had. All those years of wanting him slipped away. They hadn't been real. *This* was real. This right here.

"Tell me again."

I grinned. "I love you, Ash Talmadge."

His lips crashed down on mine, capturing those words forever. Our kissing turned frantic and desperate. As if finally admitting our feelings changed everything. Made us want to express it in every way we could. Through hands and mouths and bodies grinding against each other in the water.

"Ash," I gasped.

His cock was long and hard as I rocked my hips back and forth against it. We had bathing suits between us. So little clothing left that it would be so easy to have him inside of me. His hands were on my ass, pushing me hard down against him. As if the heat between us could boil the water, and still, it wouldn't be hot enough.

"I need you, Mia."

"Take me," I begged.

"I wanted this that first night in the hot tub."

"Show me what you wanted."

He lifted me out of the water as if I weighed nothing. My feet touched the seat we'd been sitting on, and he turned me to face away from him. Then, he bent me forward at the waist so that my ass was in the air.

I looked back at him over my shoulder and smirked.

"Mine," he growled.

"All yours."

Then, he tugged off my wet bottoms, letting them splash in the water behind us. His trunks followed them. He slipped his fingers inside of me experimentally, finding me already wet and hot for him. He moved in and out until I moaned with need.

"Ash, please, fuck."

"What would you like, Mia?" he asked. His cock slid against my ass while his fingers still drew me closer to climax.

"Fuck me," I pleaded. "I need you inside of me."

"I don't have a condom."

"I'm on the pill," I urged.

He was still working me into a frenzy while he was so calm about it all. "What if something happens?"

I looked back into his eyes, hazy and desperate. If he'd asked me that sort of question a few months ago, I would have told him to go to hell. But here with Ash now, having his children didn't sound like a bad thing. In fact, it sounded like something I wanted very much. Maybe not today. Maybe not tomorrow. But if it happened, I wouldn't regret it. Far from it.

It was that certainty that made me tell him, "I wouldn't mind if it happened with you."

His fingers stilled in surprise at those words. Then, his smile returned, big and beautiful. "I love you."

"I love you too."

He slipped his fingers out of me, and then a second

later, they were replaced by his cock. I gasped as he thrust forward deep inside of me. All thoughts of our earlier conversation evaporated. There was just the here and now. With him in love with me.

As I came apart, we both cried out into the night.

A new ending. A new beginning. And the entire world left before us.

23

SAVANNAH
SEPTEMBER 18, 2021

Mark pushed a vodka tonic with lime across the bar to me. I shot him a smile even though I was more of a whiskey drinker. He sometimes said that girls didn't actually like whiskey, that they just drank it to impress guys. Which I thought was ridiculous, but everyone else laughed when he said it. So, I probably shouldn't have taken it too seriously.

Or so I told myself as I sipped on the vodka, cringing at the sharp taste. It wasn't even a quality vodka.

Mark's friends were at the bar, surrounding us. None of them had girlfriends. They were all eternal bachelors. That was what they said at least. I called them all fuck bois since they picked up a different girl every night we went out drinking. It was the least

Wait for Always

offensive thing about them. If *boys will be boys* was a group of people, it was *these guys*.

"Let's go to another bar. This one doesn't have enough options," John said.

"Yeah. We should just head to Wet Willie's," another guy said.

Two of the other guys chimed in at the same time.

"Sure," Mark said.

He raised his hand for the tab. He was footing the entire bill tonight. Sometimes, I wondered if that was why everyone came out with him all the time. He threw around daddy's money like it was an endless waterfall.

"You ready to go, babe?"

I stared down at my full drink. I wasn't going to finish this in the next couple of minutes. I hadn't even wanted it in the first place.

"Uh, I'll leave this here," I said, setting it back on the bar.

Mark wrinkled his nose. "Just chug it. Don't waste my money."

I stared at the full glass and then back at him. "I'll get the next round then."

That made him even angrier. "You're not paying for a drink."

I laughed, trying to defuse the tension. "I used to buy drinks for myself all the time in New York. The drinks are cheaper here."

But Mark didn't like that. I should have just let it go.

He had gotten it into his head that no one was allowed to do anything without his permission. He was the life of the party. He bought the drinks. He was the entire entertainment. I wasn't allowed to order a drink, one that I actually liked, without him blowing a fuse.

"Well, this isn't New York," he said like I didn't realize that. "Now, finish the drink."

It wasn't worth the fight. I opened my throat and poured the vodka down it. At least I didn't have to taste it. Though I was already tipsy. I could hold my alcohol pretty well, but we'd been out for a few hours already.

My phone buzzed against my hip, and I fished it out of my purse as we headed toward the door.

Where are y'all? We're going to end at Lulu's. You could meet us.

My stomach flipped with anxiety at the text from Derek. He'd come in town to celebrate Ash's birthday. It wasn't until Tuesday, but since he lived in Atlanta, it was harder to do things during the week now. He'd asked me to come out with them, but I'd said no.

I hadn't seen or talked to Ash since that day when he found out about Lila and Cole's engagement. I'd decided to move on. I just wanted to forget about how much time I'd wasted with him.

With Mark, it was better. Easier. There wasn't a lifetime of baggage associated with him. We'd met on a dating app, which I'd thought was a horrible idea, but he was the first person who messaged me, and I got off of the thing as soon as we met. We hit it off so well over that first glass of wine. He hadn't pushed for more that day. Just texted and called me every single day until I was drunk on him.

But I'd told him all about what had happened with Ash. The only thing I regretted about our relationship. Now, he hated Ash and went out of his way to bring him up and make me feel guilty for having anything to do with him. Even though ... I had nothing to do with him.

It was so frustrating.

Have fun. I'm staying with Mark and his friends.

Come on! It's Ash's birthday.

I huffed. That was exactly why I wasn't going. Ash had made his choice. He hadn't chosen me. I'd known him my entire life. I'd put up with a lot of shit from him. But I couldn't do this anymore. I couldn't deal with it, and I didn't deserve to.

"Who is texting you?" Mark asked, slinging an arm across my shoulders.

I slid the phone back into my purse. "Just my brother."

I hadn't told him that it was Ash's birthday or that Derek had driven down to see him for it. In fact, I didn't bring up Ash at all. There was no point. It wasn't like Mark talked about his exes. I didn't want to talk about mine ... or whatever Ash and I had been.

Mark shot me a suspicious look. "What does he want?"

"Nothing," I lied. It was easier than explaining.

The light changed from red to green at the corner of Congress, and we headed across the street toward City Market. The guys were elbowing each other and pointing out a few of the SCAD students. And then when we were past the group of college students, there he was.

Ash Talmadge.

It had only been three months since I'd officially walked away from him, and my heart made a traitorous leap at the sight of him. He'd ditched his customary suit for khakis and a polo with boat shoes. As preppy as he was.

He looked up from the crosswalk to find me walking toward him. And the melancholic look that was on his face evaporated, and in its place was joy. Like he'd been waiting this whole time to see and talk to me. Now, I was here, and his birthday weekend was complete.

Then, Mark was there with his arm around me, pulling me closer toward him. I glanced up to see the flash of fury on his face. As if this were somehow my fault. As if I'd known Ash was going to be there in that moment, walking toward us.

Derek traipsed right up to me in the middle of the

street. "Mia! There you are!"

"Hey, Derek."

"You coming with us to Lulu's?"

"Uh ... no," I said, glancing at Mark and trying not to cringe. I shouldn't have even told Mark about Derek texting me. He was so sensitive about it all.

"Nothing, huh?" Mark growled.

"Mark ..."

He turned away from me. His smile for my brother was something out of a cartoon. He whipped it out so fast that only I realized how upset he must be underneath the veneer of charming Southern boy.

"Hey, Derek!" He held his hand out, and they shook. "We're heading to Wet Willie's. Y'all want to join?"

Derek looked to Ash, who was still looking at me. "We're out for Ash's birthday," Derek explained. "So, I'm going wherever he wants."

"We'll pass," Ash said with barely a glance in Mark's direction.

Derek clapped Ash on the back. "If you change your mind, you know where we are."

"Sure, sure," Mark said with a smile.

We crossed the street, making it to the sidewalk just as the light turned red. Mark didn't say a word as we stepped into Wet Willie's and found his friends. Tension bristled between us. His friends pretended not to notice, but we were only in there a few minutes before Mark erupted.

"What the fuck was that, Amelia?" he snarled.

I opened and closed my mouth. "I didn't know they'd be there."

"Let me see your phone."

"What?" I gasped.

"Let me see it."

"Why?"

"Were you texting him?" he demanded, grabbing my bag at my waist and digging my phone out of it.

I looked on in shock that he would have the audacity to go through my purse, but he didn't stop there. He punched in the code to my phone as if he'd done this before, as if he'd looked for evidence that I was still talking to Ash behind his back.

"Mark," I whispered in horror.

"So, you were texting Derek."

"I told you that." I grabbed my phone back with a shaky hand. "I told you he texted me."

"You said it was nothing, but he was trying to get you to meet him and Ash."

"He'd invited me when he said he was driving into town, and I declined. I said no to be with you," I said, trying to keep the tears from coming to my eyes.

"Don't cry. You're embarrassing yourself," he said callously.

Meanwhile, his friends stood around, acting as if none of it was happening at all.

I swiped at my eyes with the back of my hands. "I don't know why you're doing this."

"I saw the way you looked at him," he said low as he got into my face aggressively. "Were you thinking of going with him? Are you that desperate again, Amelia?"

"No," I hissed.

He grabbed my arm, pulling me closer. His fingers dug in hard enough to bruise. "You're an idiot for ever thinking he'd care about you. I'm the only person who will ever care about you. Do you understand?"

"Yes," I whispered.

"You should have told me about his birthday. You should have told me he'd be out. This is your fault."

I swallowed down all the words I wanted to say to him. How all those demands meant a new argument with him. This same conversation on repeat. Even though he had nothing to worry about. Even though I was never going back to Ash. None of it made sense. And yet I had to manage Mark's emotions and make him comfortable at every turn. Without him ever thinking about how that interaction hurt *me*.

"I know," I finally said.

"We should just go," Mark snapped.

"Go?"

"Yeah. This is humiliating. You're crying in the bar, texting your ex. I can't be seen with you here."

He dropped a hundred down with his friends and made some excuse I never heard. Then he had me by my upper arm and hauled me out of the bar. I didn't even object. I didn't know what to do or say. I hadn't even *done* anything.

But still, I went. I got back to Mark's house and changed into sleeping clothes.

"I'm taking a shower. Don't wait up," Mark snapped.

The bathroom door slammed shut, and I winced.

I crawled into his bed. There didn't seem to be a way to avoid this. He was mad, no matter what I did. I pulled my phone up and scrolled through my list of blocked numbers. It was a bunch of unknown numbers and then Ash Talmadge.

I glanced at the bathroom and then clicked Unblock.

Happy birthday.

Almost immediately, a text came in from him.

Thanks, Mia. It was good seeing you tonight. I miss you.

I held the phone to my chest and closed my eyes around those words. Then, I let it all go. I couldn't talk to him anymore. Not if I wanted things to work with Mark.

So, I deleted the messages, changed the passcode on my phone, and tried to sleep. But sleep evaded me as my brain went around and around on how to make sure this didn't happen again.

24

SAVANNAH
JANUARY 27, 2022

I kicked open the door to my house and dropped the samples onto a chair. I had so much work to do to get ready for the next launch. All I wanted to do was take a nap. Mark had called earlier and said he'd be at work late and not to wait up. Which I'd thought was a good thing at the time. I'd get so much work done. But now ...

My room was on the second floor of my townhouse. I stripped out of my work attire and into my Taylor Swift cardigan and sweats. Mark sort of thought it was ugly, but I wore it with pride around his house all the time.

I came downstairs and started making a pot of coffee, hoping it would give me the energy I needed to do some more work tonight, when my cell phone dinged.

Are you home?

My hand shook as I stared at the name. Ash. What the ...

Ash hadn't texted me since his birthday when I stopped answering his messages. I'd opened the floodgates with my birthday text, but I'd shut it all down. I was pretty sure Mark had tried to get in my phone after that, but he didn't know the new passcode. I never brought it up again.

I had nothing to hide, but it was the lack of privacy. And while he'd left my phone alone, everything else had gotten gradually worse. That night had been the tipping point for him grinding me under his heel. Every day since New Year's Eve, I'd been considering walking away. Then, I'd talk to someone about it, try to explain his behavior, and everyone thought I was crazy. *Mark wasn't actually like that. Mark was lovely. I should be happy to have someone like that. Everyone wanted someone like him.* Well ... maybe they could have him.

I cringed at that thought. I didn't want to leave him. I didn't know *how* to leave hm. Maybe I was the crazy one anyway. That was what he said, and everyone who knew him couldn't understand why I wouldn't love him. And I did love him. Fuck. Around and around and around in circles.

Mia?

Fuck, I shouldn't answer that question. But why was he texting me? He'd stopped months ago.

I'm home. Why?

But then I didn't get a response from him. *The fuck, Ash?*

I had too much to do tonight. I couldn't figure out what his game was.

I grabbed the box of samples and dropped the thing on the kitchen table. Material fell out in a wave. All the beautiful colors I was working on for the summer launch. Colors that I couldn't wait to get to, but tonight, I had little inspiration for it.

When the coffee was finished, I poured the entire thing into a mug with some cream and sugar and took a long sip. I needed to get some pep in my step. I probably needed … assistant designers. That thought had been racing through my mind too. While Mark and I were falling apart, the business was thriving. Summer was looking to be the biggest summer *ever*. And it made me wonder if my dream of building an empire might actually happen. Mom would certainly appreciate me opening another location in Charleston. Maybe I could escape *there*. Maybe *that* would be safe.

Then, the doorbell rang.

I wrinkled my nose in confusion. No one else was supposed to be here. Mark was gone tonight.

I set my coffee down by my samples and went to

the front door. I glanced through the peephole to make sure it wasn't a solicitor and almost fell over at the sight of Ash Talmadge on my front step. I yanked the door open.

"What are you doing here?" I blurted before I could stop myself.

Then, I got a good look at him. His shirt was rumpled. He'd lost his suit jacket, but he still wore the navy pants. His hair wasn't gelled, and it looked like he'd been running his hands through it. His eyes were red and face a mask of distress.

"Ash, are you okay?"

"Can I come in?" he croaked.

"Of course," I said, pulling the door wide.

Ash stepped inside my house. He caught one glimpse of the table full of brightly colored material and frowned. "Am I interrupting?"

"It's fine. I was planning to work all night. Try to figure out my summer designs. What's going on?"

He finally met my eyes. "My dad had a heart attack."

"Oh my God," I gasped, my hands going to my mouth. "Is he okay?"

"He's in the hospital. They have to do surgery. I don't know what the fuck to do. I don't know if he's going to make it."

"Fuck, Ash. Sit down." I directed him toward the couch, where he fell into the cushions. "Let me get you a drink."

I busied myself in the kitchen and came back out a few minutes later with some scotch in a glass. He took it but didn't drink. Just stared down into the liquid, as if it had the answers to his problems.

I took the seat next to him and put my hand on his back, rubbing easy circles there.

"I'm sorry," he said finally. "I shouldn't have barged in on you like this."

"You shouldn't be alone."

"Yeah, but ... I know Mark hates me."

I hadn't even thought about Mark. He was the last thing on my mind with this going on. "He ... does," I said, unable to argue. "But I don't hate you."

He looked up at me with surprise. "After everything, I deserve your hate, Mia."

"Let's not do this right now. That's not why you're here. I've known you my entire life. I can be here for you for this. We don't have to solve our issues tonight."

I didn't know if we even *could* solve our issues. All that mattered was that Ash was one of my oldest friends and he was in pain. It wasn't about *us*. It didn't need to be for me to be here for him.

"What do you need from me?"

Ash shook his head. "Just being here is better."

"Okay. How about I order us some dinner? You can just sit here." I glanced at the clock.

Mark wouldn't be out of work until at least midnight. When he got deep into work, I never saw him. I probably should tell him that Ash Talmadge was here, but I didn't want that fight. It wasn't sexual. It was just about our friendship. His dad was sick. He needed someone.

"All right," Ash said, and then he finally took a sip of the drink.

I ordered pizza and turned on the latest Marvel TV show. My samples were long forgotten as we sat on the couch together and ate pizza, like old times. I even managed to get a smile from him. We paused the show at one point when he got a call from his mom about his father's surgery.

"Should we go there now?" I asked.

"Is that Amelia?" I heard his mom ask.

"Yeah, I'm at her house."

"Tell her I said hello."

Ash shot me a sheepish look. "My mom says hi."

"Hi."

He stepped away and listened for a minute. "She told me not to come up there. To stay where I'm at. She'd update me if anything happens."

"You're sure? I'll go with you."

"Mom said she invited her entire charity group over, and they're praying in the waiting room. I don't want to be around that. I ..." He shook his head. "Can I just stay here?"

"Of course," I said softly.

We went back to the TV show. The tension never really left Ash. He kept glancing at his phone to see if his mom had texted or called him. She sent periodic updates, but nothing had happened still. So, I pulled out the emergency ice cream, and we dug into the pint together.

"Is this butter pecan and pistachio?" he asked in disbelief.

"I ... order a few pints from Leopold's, and they make them special for me," I said with a laugh.

"That is brilliant."

"Nothing else compares."

"Never," he agreed.

As we dived in to the season finale, I couldn't keep myself from yawning.

"Long day?" he asked.

"Yeah. Sorry," I said as I lay down on the pillow and tucked my feet up. "The business is ... flourishing. Which means long hours at the shop and not enough time to do everything."

"That sounds like a good thing."

"It is," I agreed.

He was silent another minute and then said, "I wish things were always like this with us."

"Let's not," I said again. "I don't want to talk about us. I'll get mad and kick you out, and you need me. I'm still here for you, but can we ... just pretend?" I pleaded. "Just for one day?"

Ash looked like he wanted to say so much more. I had no idea what those words were that he kept locked behind his teeth, but he finally nodded.

I was glad. I couldn't do that right now. He was

always a part of my life here in Savannah, but I didn't want to have to deal with all the years of baggage behind that statement. I could be here for him when his dad was sick, but I couldn't discuss us at the same time.

At some point, I must have fallen asleep because I felt a hand on my shoulder. "Mia."

I glanced up to see Ash still seated next to me. "Is everything okay? Your dad?"

"I haven't heard, but..."

And what he was going to say became apparently clear as the door to my townhouse opened. I jumped to my feet. And in walked Mark Armstrong.

"Hey, babe. I got off early!"

Then, he stood frozen in the doorway.

"Mark, hey," I said, trying to think of a way to fix this and finding no available option.

"What the fuck is this?" he snarled.

Panic set in, and my hands started shaking. Oh no. Oh no, no, no. I knew what was about to happen. I'd thought I'd have time to get Ash to the hospital. To find a way to tell Mark what was going on, but instead, I'd just avoided the situation and hoped it would all go away.

"Hey, man," Ash said. He came to his feet and held his hand out. "I don't know that we've officially been introduced."

"I don't need to be fucking introduced to you," Mark said. "I know what the fuck you're doing here."

Ash balked at the way Mark was talking and chanced a glance at me.

"It's nothing," I said hastily. "Ash's dad had a heart attack. He's in surgery."

"So, what the fuck is he doing here? Fucking you while he waits?"

I winced at the words. "No."

"She's my oldest friend, man. Nothing happened."

"I don't fucking need a word from you," Mark growled. "You should get the fuck out of here before I punch you."

Ash ignored Mark and faced me. "Come to the hospital with me. We should probably go."

"I ..." I whispered uncertainly.

"Amelia," Mark said, "what the fuck?"

"It's not what it looks like," I said again. "I swear we were just eating pizza and watching TV."

"So, it was a date, not just fucking," Mark accused. He'd taken another step toward me aggressively, and he was nearly in my face.

"Dude, back off," Ash said.

"Ash, don't," I whispered.

Mark laughed in his face. "You think you're so fucking tough. I know everything about you. I know that you're a piece of shit who got left at the altar and for good reason."

Ash looked like he was going to throw a punch. But I grabbed his arm and jerked him backward.

"Stop." I repeated, "Just stop."

I stepped around Ash and went to Mark. "Please, you know I would never do anything with anyone when I'm with you. Not ever."

"I don't know that. I know that you've been in love with him, and then he's fucking here."

Mark grabbed my arm the way he had that night in the bar. My memories flashed of the humiliation. The disgust on his face. The feelings of inadequacy that had plagued me for so long after. And it all came back in a rush. No one had stood up for me. No one had even said a word.

But this time, Ash did.

"What the fuck is wrong with you?" Ash snarled. He came between us in an instant. "Don't fucking touch her."

Ash and Mark were nose to nose. One wrong move would send this entire thing spiraling. I'd seen Ash fight someone before. I never wanted to see it again.

"Ash, please," I gasped. "Please ... just go."

His eyes shot to me. "Me? I should go?"

"Yes."

Mark snorted.

"It's not safe, Mia."

And I saw that he truly believed that. My cheeks heated.

"I'll be fine."

Mark pushed him in the chest. "You heard the woman. Get the fuck out. She's my girlfriend, not yours. You're not wanted here."

Ash looked back at me with such a pleading look that I wanted to go with him. But he'd ruined our chance. He'd chosen. There was nothing he could do here. As much as I wanted to be there for him through this, my relationship wouldn't survive me walking out of that door with him.

"Call Derek," I told him. "I'm sorry."

Ash shook his head once, shot a withering look at Mark, and then left. And as soon as the door closed, I knew I had made the wrong choice.

I was in too deep to do anything about it in that moment. But it was the beginning of the end.

A week later, I'd leave Mark for good and start the process of opening the new boutique in Charleston to get myself a safe way out of the mess.

25

SAVANNAH
PRESENT

The dress for the Foster Foundation charity event was a masterpiece. Even though I frequently sold outfits that I'd worn first, I was contemplating keeping this one to myself forever. It hung on the back of my closet door in a wave of red silk, and I couldn't wait to wear it tonight to be recognized for my contribution to the foundation.

I'd hired hair and makeup since I'd be in so many pictures. I already felt like a goddess, just standing around in my matching underwear set. All I had to do was slip into the dress and heels and wait for Ash to pick me up.

I took a sip of my water while I listened to Sinatra croon from my record player. My phone rang, and I grabbed it, turning the music off before answering.

"Amelia Ballentine."

"Amelia, it's Nolan Holden."

I froze in place. I'd been waiting for this call for weeks. I knew that this was all a *hurry up and wait* business, but it was still frustrating to be on the waiting end of it all.

"Hi, Nolan. It's great to hear from you."

"Good to talk to you. I want to make this a quick call. I know it's late for a Friday, but I had so many meetings today."

"It's not a problem. I was just getting ready for a charity event."

"That sounds fun. Well, I hate to be the bearer of bad news, but we had another clothing retailer come in and make an offer on the space we were negotiating."

My stomach fell. "Oh, really?"

"I'm not at liberty to discuss who it is at the time, but they're a large name brand, and they offered to pay double for the location."

I nearly choked. Double. Holy shit. "Wow. That's ... surprising."

"It's been happening all over. Big corporations are coming into these lucrative spaces and raising rent everywhere."

Which you could stop. I wanted to say it, but Nolan Holden was a businessman. It was his job to make money. Not to support local small businesses. Not when he could get double his cut just by agreeing to this. I hated it, and I knew why Marina hated it, but I understood it too. It didn't make me feel any better.

"Well, I don't think I would be able to meet that demand."

Nolan sighed. "I thought you might say that. I'm really sorry, Amelia, but we're going to have to go with the other offer. We might be able to move you into another space when one comes available. I'll be in touch if you're interested."

"Sure," I said in a noncommittal tone.

It felt like the rug had been pulled out from under my feet. And instead of falling on the floor, I fell into a never-ending pit. I made some small talk before hanging up the phone and sitting down on my bed.

The dream that I'd been working on for my empire was dead in the water. Maybe it was dramatic to feel like everything I'd worked for was over, but I couldn't stop the feeling from taking root and growing inside of me. I had my boutique here. It was in great shape, but I wanted more. I wanted to franchise the boutiques. I wanted them everywhere in the South. I wanted them everywhere. Charleston had felt like the first step to that dream coming true. And it was the first step I'd made when I had that idea of leaving Mark behind. Now, it was gone.

Maybe I didn't need to be saved from my abusive ex any longer, but I still felt like I was letting that girl down who had needed it. The shop was just a shop. It wasn't something that could eventually pay double the rent to get the prime real estate. It wasn't a conglomerate that was going to take over the world. And I hadn't realized how much I'd been relying on that dream until it felt like it was gone.

It would be easier. I could be here in Savannah with Ash. And that was that.

I sighed and flopped backward on the bed. I didn't even hear the front door open until my name was called and feet stomped up the stairs.

"There you are," Ash said with a smile. His eyes crawled down my mostly naked body. "While I am here for this attire, why aren't you dressed?"

"The world is ending."

Ash laughed. "Is that so?"

"I got a call from Nolan," I said, meeting his eyes. "He had someone else offer double to take my spot."

Ash's jaw dropped open. "And he took it?"

"Wouldn't you?"

He didn't dispute it right away, but I could see that he wanted to. We both knew that he wouldn't though. If someone was willing to pay that much money, no one was going to tell them no.

"I'll call him," he growled.

"Don't bother."

"Mia ..."

"It's done, Ash. I can't change how it happened, but it's over. I don't want you to ruin your friendship over this."

"Well, we'll figure something else out then. We can find a place here or somewhere in Charleston. He has other properties."

A tear came to my eye, and I hiccupped. "Fuck, Ash, I thought this was it."

"Oh, Mia." He sank onto the bed and pulled me into him. "This isn't the end for you or for the expansion of the boutique. I know you're going to go off and do amazing things."

I shook my head. "Maybe I'm as worthless as I thought."

He stilled. "Why would you say that?"

"I only ever get things because I know people in power. My dad, Camden, you."

"Me?"

"You got me the interview with Holden."

"And that had nothing to do with anything."

"You made the call," I reminded him. "I must not have been good enough or he would have said yes immediately before looking at other offers."

"You can't blame yourself for any of it. It's business. It didn't work out. That hardly makes you worthless. I've never heard you talk like that."

I dabbed at my eyes. "I just ... I don't know how to explain."

"Sit up. Talk to me."

I did as he said, looking into those big blue eyes. The ones that were all mine. The ones that should have been enough for all of this. But he didn't know that, some days, I was holding myself together with duct tape, string, and gum.

"Do you remember when you came to see me after your dad was sick?"

His face clouded. "Yes."

"And how upset Mark was?"

"I remember him being a douchebag and worrying that he'd hurt you." He suddenly looked terrified. "Did he?"

"Physically ... no."

"Fuck."

"It was months of him belittling me. And it sounds so ridiculous because I should have just left him. He wasn't always like that, and then by the time it got as bad as it did, I was in so deep."

"Why didn't you come to me?"

I shook my head, recoiling from him at that thought. "He hated you. We fought about you constantly."

"Of course he hated me, but I never knew why. You never talked to me."

"I know," I whispered. "But I told him everything before we dated and he hated you so much. He thought I still loved you. He went through my phone to see if we'd been messaging. He accused me of cheating. The two times we saw you, it was like my everything shut down."

Ash took my hand in his. "I had no idea. Amelia, I wish I had been there ... been better."

"It wasn't your fault. It was his. All his. And no one

believed me. But anyway, I left a week after you were here. For me, it was like Charleston was my escape plan. I was going to leave it all behind and move there to get away. The brilliant plan was the reason I had the gall to leave him."

"Ah," he said, finally understanding. "And now, it's gone. Your escape route just closed."

"And I don't need to escape you," I said quickly. "Obviously."

"I don't think you do."

"It just feels like everything shrank, and there's no way to get away. Even though I want to be here with you."

"You don't have to explain." He brought my hand to his lips and kissed them. "I love you. I understand your distress. I wish I could kill Mark Armstrong for ever making the strong, beautiful woman I love feel this way. But it's not the end. You can still do everything you want, and I'll be here every step of the way."

I leaned forward, pressing my cherry-red lips to his. "Thank you."

"For loving you?"

I laughed. "I guess so."

He held me tight until I felt the panic begin to subside. "As much as I hate to say this, we need to get you into that dress."

I rose to my feet on shaky legs and removed the red dress. I stepped into it and turned my back to him. "Zip me up?"

Wait for Always

"I'm going to unzip it and leave it on the floor later," he teased.

"I'm counting on it."

When the zipper hit the base of my spine, I turned to face Ash. He breathed in sharply in appreciation.

"You look stunning."

"Thank you," I whispered. "Is my makeup a mess?"

He shook his head. "Looks good as new."

I ran into the bathroom real quick to check and found, to my surprise, that he was right. I grabbed my clutch, stuffed my phone in it, and then followed Ash out of my house.

The Foster Foundation charity was in an event space off of River Street. We parked in the garage and took the elevator up to the ballroom floor, which had a balcony overlooking the Savannah River. The room was already full of people, and I laughed when I realized that my entire family had shown up. My dad and Kathy stood near Ash's parents. My mom, Marina, Daron, and Tye stood next to Derek and Marley. They all congratulated me a million times over when I stepped into the room.

I still hadn't had that conversation with my dad. Things had been moving too fast for me to slow down enough to deal with him. But he was there, and maybe that made him a little better than the day before. He showed up for me when it was important.

"You look beautiful, sweetheart," Dad said.

"Thanks, Daddy."

Then, we stood there for a beat too long in silence. Me waiting to see if he was going to say something more, offer to take me to lunch. But then the moment passed, and nothing happened. Neither of us knew how to bridge that gap. So, I pulled back. It wasn't my responsibility, and I couldn't do it with everything else going on.

I said hi to the rest of my family. Marina cursed Nolan's name when I told her the news. Derek and Marley insisted it was for the better and that I'd have another option. Kathy hugged me hard, knowing how much it meant to me. But it was Mom who was the ever-practical one.

"Come visit me this summer and fall back in love with the city. You'll know what to do when you get there."

I hugged her hard because she was right. She was so right.

Then, I was called up to the front for my award. I was handed a little plaque that I was excited to display at the shop and gave a quick speech, thanking everyone involved. Foster Foundation had been important to me for years. I wanted to keep making it a priority even if all the rest of my dreams failed and I never expanded. At least I'd made a difference for this.

I stepped off the stage and was ready to head back to Ash when the whole world stopped, and I struggled to breathe as Mark Armstrong appeared before me with that deadly smirk.

26

SAVANNAH
PRESENT

I hadn't seen Mark since I'd gotten my box back from him, and I'd hoped that I never would again. After the day I'd had and my escape plan closing, I was more vulnerable than ever, which was the worst possible place for me to be around Mark.

"Hello, Amelia," he said.

"Mark," I said softly. "What are you doing here?"

"It's a charity event. My family was invited, obviously."

"Obviously," I repeated.

I wanted nothing more than to walk away from him. To not stand in front of him, feeling as small as ever. All the things he'd said had come true. I hadn't amounted to anything, and I'd run right back into Ash's arms.

"And you ..." His eyes crawled down the red silk of my dress. "You look the same as always."

I straightened at those words. Had that been a compliment, or was he insulting me?

I ran my eyes down him as well. He was in a black tuxedo. The bow tie was a little askew. His blue eyes were glassy, and his dark hair had grown out just a little too long. He looked like the same Mark who had hurt me over and over again for months, but his words struck the hardest.

"Thank you," I managed.

"Have you missed me?"

I opened my mouth and then closed it. He just laughed at me.

Something in that laugh sparked a fury straight down my spine. How many times had he laughed at me? How often had he belittled and degraded me? How frequently had I let him get away with it?

I wasn't with Mark Armstrong anymore. I shouldn't have let him do it in the first place. I should have left months before I finally gave up on him. But I hadn't. I'd had to learn my worth all over again. After a few short months with Ash, I knew that I didn't deserve anything that Mark was going to throw my way.

I wouldn't shrink back. I wouldn't be made smaller. Not this time.

"Actually ... I didn't."

Mark blinked at me. "Didn't what?"

"Miss you. I didn't miss you at all."

Mark stumbled over his scoff of disbelief. "Of

course not. You're playing second fiddle to Ash Talmadge now, aren't you?"

"If you mean that he loves me, then, yeah ... he loves me."

Mark snorted. "Sure he does. Keep telling yourself that."

"I don't have to tell myself that when he tells it to me all the time."

Then, Ash appeared smoothly at my side. He wrapped an arm possessively around my waist and pressed a kiss to my neck. "You were brilliant."

I looked up at him with the brightest smile. He hadn't even acknowledged Mark when he came over to claim me openly in front of him. It was perfect.

"Thanks."

"I missed you," he told me. Then, he stole my bright red lips for his own.

Mark made a noise of protest, and Ash broke away to find him standing there.

"Oh hi, Mark," Ash said with a grin that said he knew precisely what he was doing. "Surprised to find you here."

"Why is that?" Mark ground out.

"Because I thought it was clear that you were unwelcome."

Mark's eyes rounded. "You're just a desperate piece of trash, still recovering from your bullshit with that Greer girl."

Ash met my gaze and shrugged. "That's a lot of words for him to tell me he's jealous."

I snickered, which only pissed Mark off more. He took a menacing step forward. I would have backed far away from that, but not with Ash at my side, holding me firm in my convictions.

"You fucking asshole."

Ash held his hand up, stopping Mark in his tracks. "What did you say to me the last time we met? Oh, right. She's my girlfriend, not yours. You're not wanted here." Ash reached forward and straightened Mark's bow tie with a flourish. "So, leave."

"Amelia," Mark said, redirecting his anger.

"I really don't want to hear it, Mark. I dealt with enough while we were together. We broke up. I left. No one believed me about you, but now, maybe they will." I gestured to the crowd of people surreptitiously watching our altercation. "Maybe I wasn't crazy after all."

I didn't wait for him to say more. I took Ash's hand and walked away from my ex. My hands were shaking with anger at the fact that he'd shown up and the terror of standing up to him. I'd always wondered if I had done that when we were alone, would he have hit me? So instead, I'd stayed small and quiet and submissive. I didn't have to be those things ever again.

"He wanted a fight," Ash said.

"He did. I didn't want to give him the satisfaction."

"Plus, I don't want to ruin my new tux." Ash ran his

Wait for Always

hands down the front of the suit. "Would have been criminal to get his blood all over it."

I laughed sharp and abrupt at the words. "Since when did you become a comedian?"

"I don't start fights, Amelia, but I damn sure would have ended it."

I'd seen him do it before, and I was glad that it hadn't gotten to that point. I didn't need him to defend me. I'd done that on my own. But oh, it had been sweet to see Ash do it as well.

"He's not worth my peace."

"It's good to hear you say that." He offered me his hand, and when I placed it in his, he kissed it. "I don't want anyone to make you feel less than ever again."

"You never have."

"Ah, I think I have," he said softly. "In the past, I made you feel that way."

"Not like Mark."

"Maybe not, but not good either. And I don't want you to ever have to go through that again."

"I love you," I said, kissing him.

"I love you too." He took my hand and pulled me toward the dance floor. "Now, dance with me."

This wasn't a debutante ball. The music was slow, but no one was waltzing around the floor. I put my arms around Ash's neck, and his slid around my waist. We swayed to the music in perfect sync, as if we'd been doing this our whole lives. I rested my cheek against his suit and closed my eyes, relishing the moment.

Today had been trying, and I wanted this to stretch out forever.

But I couldn't be that lucky.

After the slow song ended, the music turned upbeat again, and we moseyed off the dance floor. Ash went to get me a drink, and I headed back toward my family. Kathy nudged my dad. He made an exasperated face at her and then intercepted my steps before I could reach everyone else.

"Hi, sweetheart," he said.

"Uh, hi, Dad."

It was sometimes hard to believe he was this high-powered attorney. He could make the world reshape itself around him in the court room. But just having a conversation where he wasn't in charge, where he couldn't anticipate the next argument, set him off. He didn't want to be standing here and figuring this out with me. I could tell before he'd even said hello.

Which put me on edge.

I was his daughter. I'd learned my debate skills from him. I knew a reluctant opponent when I saw one. Those skills hadn't always helped me in my career or romance, but they helped me here with my dad.

"What is it?" I asked with a sigh. "Spit it out."

His nose crinkled. "I was wondering if you had interest in meeting me for lunch next week."

"Do you actually want to get lunch with me, Dad? Or did Kathy push you into this?"

"I have a big case coming up. I don't have a lot of

time. But I can always make time for my daughter."

I laughed. "You are unbelievable."

His eyes darkened. "Amelia …"

"No. Just listen to yourself. You haven't made time for me at all."

"I'm here, aren't I?"

"I was getting an award. That makes you look good. Just like when I opened the store. That was more about you than it was ever about me. If you wanted to put in effort for something other than the law firm, you would. We all know where your priorities lie."

"That isn't true."

"Very believable," I countered. "What an argument."

He met my anger with his own. "It isn't as if you've put in effort."

"Shocking to find out, Dad, but I'm your child. You're the parent. I am going to match your energy. I see Mom more than you, and she doesn't even live here. Kathy comes by the store all the time to help."

"I don't have the luxury of helping."

"I wouldn't expect you to, but I still see Mom more. She calls. She checks in. She drives up to see me. She invites me over. She doesn't even *live* here!"

"Well, we can't all be as perfect as your mother."

I snorted. "Oh good, deflection. Excellent. We're done. I don't want to have this conversation anymore."

"Amelia," he tried again, stepping into my path before I could bolt. "We should put this petty business behind us. You're my daughter. We should make time to see one another."

My anger flared white hot. Today was not the day to test me. After the call with Nolan and then the confrontation with Mark, I didn't have any bullshit left in me. And I'd spent years with this pent-up frustration. I wouldn't hold it back anymore. Not when I had just said I would no longer sacrifice my peace.

"Why would I want to spend time with you?"

"I'm your father."

"Great. That doesn't mean I owe you my time. You have put no effort in for years. Now, everyone is forcing you into a relationship with me. I saw Kathy push you forward. Mom told me we needed to move past this. But we don't, and I don't plan to."

"What is all this even about?" he demanded.

I blinked at him in shock. "It's not enough that you don't put any effort in and I'm tired of it?"

"It started long before that, Amelia."

"Maybe it's because you cheated on my mom and ruined our family," I spat at him.

He took a step back in shock.

Ash appeared at my side then. He put a reassuring hand on my back. "Mia," he said softly.

I sank back into that touch. I'd gone too far. My dad looked distraught at those words. I didn't know why since they were true and he'd had fifteen years to get used to the idea that he was a cheating scumbag. That he'd wrecked our family and shown no remorse for it.

Wait for Always

"You haven't acted like a dad in years," I whispered, my throat closing as tears threatened to fall. "I don't owe you anything."

"Okay," my dad said. "I respect your wishes ... if that's how you feel."

Then, he walked back to Kathy, who touched his shoulder. He shrugged it off and sat down at one of the tables with his back to her. Everyone was looking at me now. Kathy and Mom had mirroring sad eyes. They'd wanted us to reconcile, and no matter how many times I'd told them I didn't want that, they'd still pushed. And now, we were here. With the truth hanging in the room around us and both of us worse off.

"I want to go home," I told Ash.

He nodded. "Of course. Let me get your purse."

Ash spoke with Derek for a few minutes before grabbing my purse and following me out. I sank into the passenger seat of his car. I was glad when he pulled up to his house a few minutes later. The tears didn't come until I was safely tucked against him in his bed. He ran his fingers through my hair.

My dreams were in the gutter.

My relationship with my father was shattered.

But at least I had Ash.

"We'll get through this, Mia," he told me soothingly. "It's going to be okay."

"I know," I lied.

"We can do this together."

That, at least, I believed.

27

CHARLESTON
PRESENT

Mom parked in front of my house. Ash reached for the handle of my suitcase and carried it down the stairs.

"You're not going to convince me to stay?" I asked when he reached me at the bottom of the stairs.

He shot me a curious look. "Why? I'll be there this weekend."

"Yeah, but ..."

He set the suitcase down and pulled me close to him. "You want to do this. You need to do this. I will support you in every way I can as long as it means, at the end of the day, you're mine." He paused a heartbeat and then asked, "You're mine?"

I nodded. "Of course I am."

"Then, go to Charleston. Find your passion again. I'll miss coming home to you every day, but I'm not holding you back."

"Okay," I whispered and then flung my arms around his neck. "Every weekend?"

"Every weekend," he confirmed. "As long as you'll have me."

"Get in the car already!" Marina shouted from the parked car.

I laughed and hefted my backpack onto my shoulder. Daron jumped out of the back and opened the trunk for my suitcase, which barely fit in my mom's car with everyone else's stuff. Tye grumbled something about how we were all going to be squished together, but Marina elbowed him and told him to shut up.

"You ready, honey?" Mom asked.

"Yeah. You're sure it's okay I come and stay for a while?"

Marina had offered her place, but Mom's house was on the water, and I felt like I needed that. My old room that I used to stay in when I visited as a kid. It would feel like old times.

"I'm sure," Mom said. "It'll be great to have you."

"Then, I'm ready."

I threw my arms around Ash again, and he kissed me for an embarrassingly long time. Long enough that my cousins started to make fun of us. I pulled away with a laugh.

"I'll see you soon," I told him.

"Not soon enough."

Then, I was in the passenger seat of the car, and we were pulling away from Savannah. Sasha was handling the store while I was gone. Kathy had promised to help wherever she was needed. And I was going to spend the time in Charleston figuring out my next move.

The two-hour drive felt like I was driving away from my entire life. I thought that feeling would go away when I got into Charleston, but it lingered. My cousins hugged me and headed out, promising to hang out. Then, I was back in my childhood room, staring out at the water.

Time seemed to pass in a haze of spending time on the water, weekends with Ash, and wandering the city that I loved. I wanted to find a new place to have a shop, but I didn't even know what I was looking for. And in realizing that I didn't know what I wanted, I investigated what I actually wanted rather than just what might fall easily into my lap. And I didn't find it.

Mom came outside after I'd been there a few weeks. I was sitting on the Adirondack chair with a sketch pad in my hand. She set down a glass of sweet tea for me.

"How's it going?"

"Well … it's going."

She smiled as she sank down next to me. "I love seeing you with a sketchbook in your hand. It reminds me of when you were a kid and designed clothes for your Barbies."

I laughed. "I forgot about that."

"Yeah. They were terrible, but everyone starts somewhere. I think you got the idea from me painting.

You started asking for art supplies after you stumbled into my studio."

"I don't remember that. Well, I remember your studio, but not the rest."

"It was the cutest. Do you know how often I went to the art store and the fabric store for you?"

"I suspect a lot."

She nodded. "Every weekend. Your dad would always be like, 'We don't need more scraps of fabric,' but I couldn't help it. Do you remember your first sewing machine?"

"The one from the attic?"

"Yep. Your grandmother's. You cried when I said you could use it if you were careful."

"I did?" I asked in a whisper.

"And when I bought you a new fancy one, you actually got mad at me."

I set down the designs I'd been working on. "I remember that. I was attached to the old one. I still have it in my house and use it."

"Your grandmother would love to hear that."

"I bet she would."

Grandma had died when I was young. I had basically no memories of her, but I had her sewing machine, and that had sustained my young heart.

"What are you working on anyway?" I handed the sketchbook to my mom, and she flipped through the pages. "These are amazing, Amelia."

"I haven't found the new store yet, but I did find a

new source of inspiration from being in town. I'd been struggling with creativity for the last year. I felt like I was recycling all my old designs even though the clothes could barely stay on the rack." I shrugged and took back the notepad. "But here, without the constant struggle of retail, my brain just unlocked."

"Maybe that means something."

"Yeah," I muttered.

"Like you should be a bit more hands off with the store anyway."

"Maybe."

"You're going to find a second location," she told me. "Or ... maybe you'll find someone to handle the day-to-day and spend more time designing. You'll figure it out. You always do."

"Thanks, Mom."

We were silent for a while. Just enjoying the summer sunshine and the crisp, cold sweet tea. It was a perfect day. And I missed Ash. He'd gone home a few days ago, and though we video-chatted every night and texted all day, it was never enough.

"I miss Ash."

"I thought you would. You've always loved that boy."

"Always," I agreed wistfully.

"So, why are you still here?"

"The store ..."

My mom shot me a look. "You can't stay here forever. You're welcome as long as you want, but you still can't stay. You love that boy, and y'all deserve to be together after all this time."

"But I'm not done."

"Give yourself another week. You'll find the place if you find the place, Mia. It doesn't have to be today or tomorrow."

She was right. That was why it was so annoying. I'd found clarity in the silence of Charleston. But I was running from everything that felt difficult. That put strain on the one good thing that was still there for me in Savannah.

"And you should talk to your father."

I jerked my head to the side. "What?"

She held her hand up to keep me from continuing. "I know you don't want to, but we should talk about it."

"There's nothing to talk about."

"Unfortunately, there is. I've let it go on long enough, but we need to talk, Mia."

"About what? Dad? I don't want to talk about him."

She reached out and touched my hand. "It didn't all happen the way that you think."

"He didn't cheat on you?"

"Well, I suppose he did," she said softly.

I jumped to my feet. "Then, that's all I need to know!"

"Amelia, sit down and listen to me," she said, raising her voice.

I slowly sank back into my seat. I'd never heard my mom yell at anyone but my dad. And even then, that had only been before the divorce. She hadn't spoken to him above something civil since then. This must be serious.

"Okay. I'm sitting."

My mom took a breath. "Your dad asked for a divorce."

"What? No, you divorced Dad."

"I know," she said. "Eventually. But at first, when you were in elementary school, your dad asked for a divorce. We were over it already. We didn't love each other. We hadn't in a long time. Not the way we should have. Just enough to make it work in public. So, he tried to divorce me, and I said no. I wanted to stay together for you and your brother."

My cheeks heated at that admission. It would have saved us a lot of strife if she'd just said yes. Years of fights and yelling if that had just happened a few years earlier.

"It's not your fault," she said immediately.

"I didn't think it was."

"Good." She nodded. "Good. Anyway, I told him I'd stay until you graduated, and then we could part ways. But to stay together, we both agreed we'd have an open relationship."

I wrinkled my nose. "What?"

She bit her lip. "See why I didn't tell you this when you were twelve? There was no way to explain this. I feel strange, even telling you now. We promised we wouldn't tell."

Wait for Always

"Jesus, Mom."

"I'm not ashamed of it. It was the best thing for our marriage if we wanted to stay together, and I did. So, we both started seeing other people. But we were up front about it. We always knew who the other person was with. The communication was good. I knew he was with Kathy. I started to see the signs that it was getting serious, I think, before he did."

"You *knew* he was with Kathy. How young *was she* when they first met?"

Mom sighed. "Twenty."

"Holy fuck. Gross!"

"Yes, we ... argued quite a bit about it at first."

"They didn't get married until she was twenty-three. So, they were together for three years without us knowing?"

"Yes."

"And you were okay with it?"

"Yes," she repeated.

"So, what happened?" I asked, unable to comprehend how this could possibly have worked. I'd thought my mom loved him too much to ever let him be with someone else. And now, she was saying that the opposite was true.

"Well, he lied, and I found out from Kathy."

My heart sank. "Oh."

"He was with her before I agreed to the open relationship."

"Fuck."

"Yeah. It was ... it was the breaking point for me. I'd watched him fall in love with someone else. I was even happy for them, although concerned that she was too young and how that would affect y'all later. But I wasn't interfering. I was seeing other people too. Then, Kathy told me, and it shattered everything. The trust was gone. I never trusted him again. So, I told him I wanted the divorce, and he accepted. Married Kathy almost immediately after it was finalized."

"I remember," I muttered. "I thought it was disgusting that he'd done that to you. Thought he must have been cheating for a long time."

"Not quite, but ... in the end, it didn't matter."

"That's horrible! That's a worse story."

"No," she said quickly. "I told you this against your father's wishes so that you can see that we're all human. We all make mistakes. In hindsight, I can see that I should have cut my losses and left him a lot sooner. Maybe he wouldn't have cheated if I'd agreed. Maybe he would have. I don't know. But I don't blame him for everything anymore, Amelia. I blame myself too. We don't get along, but we're not hostile. And I never blamed Kathy. I'm glad they're still happy. I don't want you to give him all the blame either."

"But he still ruined your marriage."

"Our marriage was ruined long before then," she admitted. "It's not fun to talk about. I still wish it had ended a different way, but I don't want you to resent him for it either."

I was quiet for a long time after that. I didn't know what to say. This didn't completely change how I felt about what had happened to me, growing up. It was still my dad's fault. It was just now also my mom's fault. Everyone was at fault. Even Kathy. Though hard to blame her when the age gap was so big and she was only twenty. The whole thing was a mess, and standing on the outside of it all was me and Derek.

I wished he were here to hear that story too. To realize what had all actually gone down. But he'd gotten over it years ago. He'd let it all go somehow while I'd hung on, angry and grieving the death of something that had never been perfect.

"Thank you for telling me," I said finally.

She squeezed my hand. "I love you, honey. I don't like to see you hurting. But I won't let you stay here and make a mistake either."

"I know." I nodded my head. "I'm not going to. The last thing I want is to lose Ash."

"Are you sure he knows that?"

I bit my lip. "I think so."

"You'd better be sure."

28

CHARLESTON
PRESENT

My bag was packed and waiting for me at the door to my mom's house. Ash would be here in a few hours. I hadn't told him that I was going home with him. I wanted it to be a surprise.

I'd spent the last few days taking my mom's advice. I set my sketch pad aside during the day and looked up locations online to go and check at. They'd all been a bust. Something wasn't quite right. I couldn't put my finger on it, but nothing was working for me. So, I was going to go back to Savannah and give myself the time to figure it out. I was in no rush after all.

I didn't need to escape anymore. I needed to do this the right way and for the right reasons.

I had lunch with Marina near her office on King Street. I'd avoided the heart of the city. It was mostly shop upon shop of name brands that I adored but wasn't quite me. I wanted something small and local. Something with more heart.

But today, I decided to walk with all the summer tourists on the peninsula. I trekked past all the well-known brands with a smile. I wanted to be them one day. If I could get my big start. And so I didn't begrudge them stealing the start I wanted. I knew my time would come.

Then, when I almost reached Broad, I turned onto a side street. My eyes lit up as I realized this was a little more artsy, a little trendier, and the shops ... the shops were like my boutique. There were still tourists roaming the streets, going in and out of the businesses.

I stepped in and out of the shops, purchasing new clothing, two bags, a wallet, and a handful of jewelry. With my mood lifted, I turned the corner and saw the empty building next to the one I'd just walked out of. It was an all-white front with large, open windows. I stepped up to the front door and peered inside to find an exposed brick interior.

My heart stuttered at the sight. The hardwood floor and open floor plan and modern fixtures. A sign was up on the front with the name of the company renting the place and a number.

"Oh my God," I whispered.

My fingers shook as I called the number and spoke to the agent. It was still available. I could get in to see it after five. I made an appointment to do just that and hung up, feeling hope blossom back in my stomach for the first time since I'd arrived in Charleston.

"Your suitcase is packed," Ash said when he entered Mom's house.

"Yes. I'm going home with you."

His eyebrows shot up. "What? Since when?"

"Since a couple days ago. I wanted it to be a surprise."

"You're coming home? But I thought you were still looking for a place."

"I am," I said. "Actually, I'm looking at one tonight. Go with me?"

"Of course. I'm still confused."

I reached on my tiptoes and kissed him full on the lips. "I was running. I might have been trying to find myself again, but I was scared about all of it. I wanted that escape, even when I knew I never needed one from you. I wanted you here and me here and everything here."

"Well … we could be here sometimes," he offered.

"Maybe. But on the day I got here, I realized that it's not home. Savannah is home." I paused and looked up at him tentatively. "You're home."

He swept me up into his arms and swung me in a circle. "Say it again."

"You're home," I told him as I slid down his body

and kissed him again. "And I want to come home with you."

"Move in with me."

I laughed. "Okay."

"Okay? Really?"

"Yeah. I want that. We'll sell my townhouse."

He snorted. "No, we will not. You'll rent it. What do you think I do for a living?"

I couldn't stop grinning. "All right, fine. We'll rent it. But I can move in with you?"

"I want nothing more. We'll convert a guest bedroom into an office for you. Then, you can manage the business from home too. You don't have to go in every day if you don't want to."

"I can practically walk from your house to the shop," I countered.

"On days when it's too hot to walk then."

"I can't believe this. We're really moving in together."

"We really are," he said, twirling me in place and then drawing me into him.

I kissed him again and then took his hand. "Come on. My appointment is soon. We can go out to eat downtown afterward."

Ash drove us to the shop on a side street off of King Street, parallel parking nearby. His eyes lit up when he saw the place. "Is this it?"

"Yep. I was shopping and stumbled upon it. It's not

being managed by any of the main real estate companies. I never would have found it."

"It has a lot of potential."

"I thought so too."

The real estate agent appeared then, opening the front door and letting us inside. My whole body tingled as soon as I entered. As if a spark of electricity had whipped down my spine. The place had an energy that I couldn't even begin to explain. It was ... perfect.

Ash assessed it with an eye for real estate. He was a professional after all. And I let him ask all the questions of the agent that seemed pertinent while I wandered through the place and imagined racks of clothing, a cash register at the back, and table displays. I walked into the back and saw the storage space and office. Very similar to what I had in Savannah.

"How much again?" I asked the agent.

She told me what the people were asking. Which was utterly shocking. It was less than what Nolan had been offering on the coast. And off King Street, it had to be a steal. Ash asked more questions, trying to determine if that was a standard price or if it was cheaper for a reason.

But I was already sold.

This was it.

This was the place.

"Can you send the contract over for me to look at? I'll get back to you next week."

The agent nodded. "I'd be happy to. A place like

this doesn't stay on the market for long. It's only been listed for a few days."

"I understand," I said.

But there was something else I needed to do first.

I opened the door into Ballentine Law and walked straight to the back. The assistant looked up and smiled at the sight of me.

"Well, aren't you a pleasant surprise?"

I brightened for her, and she told me to go right in.

I opened the door to my dad's office and said, "Knock, knock."

Dad looked up from his desk and then startled at my appearance. "Amelia? Is everything all right?"

"Actually, it is."

"Well, come in."

I stepped into the well-lit interior of my father's office. It was the same as it always had been with large, dark bookshelves on either side and his enormous desk at the center of the room in front of a large window that looked over the river beyond. He had two overstuffed chairs before his desk and two more on either side of the door to use if he had to meet with more than a few clients.

I perched on the edge of one of the chairs instead of sitting.

"How was Charleston?" he asked. "When did you get back?"

"It was ... enlightening. I got back yesterday with Ash."

My dad smiled. "I like that boy."

"So do I. We're moving in together. He hired movers to pack up my townhouse."

"That's great to hear, Amelia. Wedding bells in your future?"

I laughed. "Don't get ahead of yourself. We've not been together that long."

"Well, it'll all happen in time. He should know that he has my blessing, of course."

"I don't think he needs it, but I'm sure he'd be happy to hear that." I reached into my bag and removed a stack of paperwork. The real reason I'd come to his office. "Here."

I dropped the stack on his desk.

He looked down at it in confusion. Then, his lawyer brain went into full effect, and he thumbed through the pages.

"Think you could look at that and tell me what I should change?"

"This is a contract for a commercial property in Charleston."

"It is."

My dad glanced up in surprise. "I thought you and Ash were moving in together."

"We are."

"In Savannah?"

"Yep."

My dad's confusion continued. "Then, what is this?"

"I'm opening another boutique. I found the perfect location, and the rent is a satisfactory rate. If the contract looks good, then I'll sign and spend the summer setting it up."

"So ... you're going to run it from here."

"That is still in the works. I don't want to leave Ash, but this is my dream."

"I'd be happy to look at it. I want you to follow your dreams."

"Thank you."

It was an olive branch. Ash could have had any one of his lawyers look at it. I could have called Derek. But I wanted my dad to do it. I needed something to try to fix what was broken between us.

My dad frowned and looked down at the paperwork again. "I'm glad you're here, Amelia. I wanted to apologize for what happened at your charity event. But then you were in Charleston, and I didn't know how to talk to you about it."

"Mom did," I admitted.

He winced. "I'm sure that was colorful."

"It was actually. She told me everything about what happened with Kathy and the open relationship. Which ... ew. I see why y'all didn't tell me to begin with. I wouldn't have understood. I still don't understand, if I'm honest."

"I love Kathy," he said softly. "I knew that I shouldn't love her, but I did, and I still do. I've never … I've never hurt her like I hurt your mother. I never would."

"I know."

And the first realization hit me. He'd hurt my mom. It had been wrong. But he'd never hurt my bonus mom. I loved her so much, too, and I didn't want anything to happen to her. But she never would have been in my life if they hadn't divorced.

"I'd really like to find a way to begin mending this. You're my baby girl."

"I don't think it will happen overnight or anything, but maybe we can start with the contract." I smiled shyly back at him as I stood. "See where this all takes us."

He nodded once. "I'd like that."

"This is my queendom, and I am its queen," Sasha announced as she stepped foot into the mayhem of the new store.

I snorted. "You're ridiculous."

"In the best way."

"Well, obviously," I said.

Once the terms had been finalized and the contract

Wait for Always

had been signed, I'd been in full-tilt planning mode. The biggest impediment was how I was going to train people to run the place while I was still in Savannah. And that was fixed by my Sasha. She'd volunteered to move to Charleston and handle day-to-day operations there. Meanwhile, she trained up a new manager for the Savannah store so that I could also work from here.

And today was my official move-in day. I had boxes upon boxes of clothes. Not everything for the launch coming this fall, but all the extras from the Savannah store as well as the first arrivals for the fall line. Also all the equipment and racks and tables and counter. Everything to run a functioning business.

It was the second move-in day in a matter of months. I'd officially left my townhouse and into Ash's much larger house. I didn't regret it one bit. I had so much love for that townhouse that had gotten me through my twenties, but this was the right move. It was exactly where I wanted to be.

"One, two, three," Ash said, and then he and Daron lifted the table for the cash register together.

It was a hefty thing with a white marble top that I'd found at an antique store. I'd painted the bottom a shiny gold to match the rest of the store.

I dived in to the moving van, lifting equipment into the store until someone forced me to stand in place and direct people. I was doing just that when my dad of all people walked inside, holding a chair.

"Where does this need to go?"

My jaw nearly hit the floor. "Dad?"

"Hey, sweetheart."

"What are you doing here?"

He set the chair down with a huff. "I took the day off work. I wanted to help. Kathy came with me too."

I blinked. "You took time off *work*?"

My dad didn't take off work. He had one vacation a year, and that was it. He'd done it that way forever. When we went to Charleston, Dad would always come the first week, and the rest of the summer, it was just us kids with Mom. He used to even go in when he was sick. Not anymore, but once upon a time.

"Yeah. I thought it'd be nice. Kathy was excited."

"Hey, honey!" Kathy said, rushing in and hugging me. She held a lamp away from her body. "Glad we're here."

"I'm glad you're here too."

"This goes in the back, right?" she asked, pointing at the chair my dad had carried in.

"Yeah."

"Come on, Doug," Kathy said. She gestured for Dad to follow her to the back.

My mom smiled at me as I stared after them.

"Happy?"

"I can't believe he's here."

"He called me and asked when we were doing it."

"Dad called? Not Kathy?"

She nodded. "That's right. It's almost like you

reaching out fixed something that had long been broken."

"I guess so," I whispered.

Ash came over then after setting the table down. He kissed my cheek. "This is going to go so fast with so much help."

"It is. I can't believe it."

"Believe it. We all love you."

I laughed as he smacked my ass as he walked by. I spent the rest of the afternoon directing people. Until it was just me and Ash, crashed down on the velvet green couch I'd reupholstered for the room. He slipped an arm around my shoulders and kissed my cheek.

"Stay here. I have a surprise."

"A surprise?"

"A welcome gift."

"What?" I asked as he dashed off. "I don't need a welcome gift."

"I disagree," he called.

Then, he returned with a large package in his hands and offered it to me. I gave him a curious look and then tore into it. I gasped as I held a record ... the record we'd listened to that night back in New York. Frank Sinatra.

"Oh, Ash, I love it."

"Good," he said as he took my hands and pulled me to my feet. He walked me to the table where the register would sit. "Because I have something else."

And sitting on its own table that I hadn't even seen in all the madness was an antique record player.

"Oh," I gasped.

I pulled out the record and set it on the player. I pushed down the needle, and suddenly, "The Way You Look Tonight" began to filter into my empty store. He took my hand again and guided me out onto our open dance floor.

The waltz came to us as easy as breathing. We'd been doing it all our lives. And here, in this moment, I couldn't imagine being with anyone else. He pulled me in tighter and stroked my back as the world drifted away.

We might have taken a long way to get here.

But the road had absolutely been worth taking because I ended up here with him.

Like I'd always wanted.

29

CHARLESTON
PRESENT

There was no ribbon cutting. The mayor didn't show up. The fanfare was minimum. But none of that mattered on the opening of my second boutique. All that mattered was the line forming around the block to get inside.

"Ready?" Sasha asked me excitedly.

I nodded, biting my lip and trying to keep my hands from shaking. I flipped the sign to *Open* and turned the lock for the first official day of Ballentine in Charleston.

"Welcome to opening day!"

Everyone in line cheered.

The first customers burst into the room, and suddenly, it was like any other day. We had new cashiers ready to go. Sasha was in charge of everyone while I was just there to help. Especially since so many people were waiting to get in. We actually had to stop the store from being rushed and only let in as many people as the fire marshal allowed. But at least the fall weather was more conducive for waiting outside than the summer heat.

"This is insane," Marina said when she finally got into the building later that day.

Her office was only two blocks over. Anytime I was in town, I'd only be around the corner from her. I liked that a lot.

"Isn't it?"

She hugged me and then picked up a maroon dress. "Is this my color?"

"Girl, every color is your color."

"Flattery will get you everywhere," she said. "But yellow and orange are not flattering on me."

I laughed. "Noted. I bet you rock all the fall colors though."

"I do," she said with no shame.

She tried on half of the stuff in the store already, but still, she made a purchase and walked out with a skip in her step. Anything to help opening numbers. Which were already looking to be record-breaking. The only day bigger was St. Patrick's Day, and really, would anything compare to that level of insanity? Maybe a college football Saturday when I got up the nerve to continue my empire.

We were near to close. All the new cashiers were wide-eyed and excited to see so much business. It wouldn't always be like this. There would be slow

Wait for Always

days, like any retail establishment, but today, it was perfect.

Right before close, the bell over the door chimed one more time, and I looked up to find Nolan Holden in my boutique.

I smirked at him and sauntered over. "Well, hello there."

"Amelia," he said with a smile. "I wanted to come and see the new place. Pleased to see your success."

"Why, thank you. Having regrets?"

"A little," he admitted with a cheeky wink. "But I can see this is probably better for you anyway."

"I think so too."

"Well, welcome to Charleston. I'm sure I'll be seeing you around."

"Thanks, Nolan. It means a lot."

He smiled and nodded before departing. He'd made the right choice for him, and this was undoubtedly the right choice for me. If the first day was any indication, my clothes were going to do just fine in this city.

Finally, the last person paid, and I turned the sign from *Open* to *Closed*. Sasha cheered, and the final cashier flopped down on the couch in the corner. We still had to close out the register, but it was official. I was here in Charleston. And I wasn't leaving anytime soon.

A knock on the door pulled me from our celebrations, and I found Ash Talmadge stepping inside.

"Hey, beautiful," he said with a smile.

I rushed to him, throwing my arms around his neck and kissing him full on the mouth. "I had the best day."

"I like to hear that."

"Nolan showed up."

He chuckled. "Really? Did you rub your success in?"

"A little."

"As you should. He's going to wish he'd gotten you into his space when he could."

I grinned and pushed him slightly. "Nah, he's a good businessman. I'm glad he stopped by to see it for himself."

"That's how he gets you," he said with a laugh. "I know you have to finish up, but could I steal you before the party tonight?"

"That's not for two hours."

My family had cleared out the Hartage Boating building for the night and was throwing a huge celebratory party for the store.

"Go on, you two lovebirds," Sasha called. "You put me in charge. I can handle it here."

"You're sure?" I asked.

"Positive. Get out of here."

I held my hands up. I wouldn't argue with her if that was what she wanted. So, I let Ash draw me out of my new boutique with the big white sign that read *Ballentine* in all caps. I sighed with pleasure at the sight of it.

"Where are we going?" I asked him.

"Oh, not too far from here."

He took my hand, and we strolled down King Street as the sun fell lower on the horizon. Even though I'd spent all summer back and forth between Savannah and Charleston, I felt like our relationship was stronger than ever. Before I knew it, six months had passed. It was as if it had always been this incredible. As if we'd always been meant to be together.

Ash turned toward a more residential area, and I gave him a suspicious look.

"What is this?"

He shrugged, and we kept walking closer and closer toward the water. Then, finally, he stopped in front of a pink house. The siding was all baby pink with white trim and a white picket fence around the whole thing. It needed some love, but I could see under it all that the bones were good. Not too big, but not too small. In a perfect location.

It had a *For Sale* sign in the front lawn.

My suspicion grew stronger. "Ash?"

"Well, what do you think?"

"What do I think of what?"

"The house."

"I think ... it's a house. Why are we looking at it?"

He pushed open the fence and led me up the walk. He pulled up an app on his phone and then input a code into the box at the front. The lock turned, and he pushed open the front door.

"Ash?" I repeated with slight panic in my voice. "Tell me you didn't buy a house."

"Okay. I didn't buy a house."

I breathed a sigh of relief and entered the house. It was ... stunning on the inside. Maybe needed a little renovation, but the hardwood was original, and the fireplace was massive. The whole place felt like *home*.

"Yet," he added.

I whipped around. "What?"

He smirked. "I mean, I haven't bought it *yet*. You think I'd do that before making sure you loved it?"

I gaped at him. "But ... your job is in Savannah. We don't need a Charleston house."

"No, *we* need a Charleston house," he told me. "For when we come up for business all the time and when we come to see your family and when we want to get away from Savannah. Then, we have our own place."

"Oh my God," I whispered. "You're serious."

"I remember coming up to Charleston with you every summer as kids. I have all these fond memories of the place. I'd love to be able to give us that again. To give ... our kids that someday," he said, his voice going soft.

Tears came to my eyes at that admission. "I've always wanted that too."

"So, let's make it happen. Walk around. See if you

like it. Because I want a life with you, Mia. I want this to only be the first step of a long list."

"You have a list?" I teased as I stepped up to him.

"With you? I want everything."

Then, he kissed me. The world slipped away in what would be *our* Charleston house. The place I'd stay when I had to work for the business. The place he'd stay when he came to see me when I got bogged down in work. The place we'd stay when we came up with the kids for the summer.

Because that was the ultimate goal.

Waiting for always was so worth it.

EPILOGUE

CHRISTMAS EVE, FOUR YEARS LATER

It was a mild Christmas Eve, and the store was closing early.

"Go home," I told Jessica, the new Savannah store manager. "I'll lock up."

"Okay," she said excitedly. "I was supposed to meet my boyfriend anyway."

I waved her off and finished up. I had a missed call from Ash, but we'd agreed to meet at Leopold's when I was done. The office was closed on Christmas Eve, so he'd had the kids all day. I was certain he was dying for me to get there.

I locked the door up and then strolled down Broughton Street toward the ice cream parlor we'd been going to all our lives. I was almost to the door when I recognized faces. Marley, Josie ... and *Cole Davis*. My heart sped up. Oh dear, I knew what that meant.

I picked up my pace, nearly running right into Lila Greer. I didn't falter or miss a step or say a word to her. Though Lila clearly saw me and smiled softly. I hurried past and straight into Leopold's. Ash stood with our two kids, James and Katie.

"Sorry I'm late," I said in a rush as I threw myself into his arms.

"Glad you made it."

"Mommy!" James cried.

I gave him a big kiss and then lifted little Katie into my arms. James was the mirror image of his father. Even named James Asheford Talmadge V. In the end, we'd gone with tradition.

"Happy birthday, beautiful boy!" I called. "How does it feel to be three?"

"Excellent," he said with a cheeky smile that was so like his father.

"Mommy, when am I three?" Katie asked.

She was my mini me. Just two years old and already talking more than James ever had at that age. A girl was *so* different than a boy, and I loved having one of each. Just like me and Derek.

"You'll be three next year."

Katie stuck out her bottom lip. "I want to be three today too."

I laughed. "That's not how birthdays work. But you both get ice cream. What flavor are you picking out?"

We all grabbed our cones. Mine butter pecan and pistachio, of course. Ash had gone for chocolate chip.

James and Katie fought over the various versions of chocolate before deciding on the standard flavor. Katie would do anything to get what James was eating. Or anything James was doing ever.

I waited until we had the kids safely at an outdoor table before looking to Ash. "Well, how was that?"

"How was what?"

"I saw Lila walk out of here and Cole Davis on the street with Mars and Josie."

"It was fine," he admitted. Then, he reached for my hand and kissed my fingers. "It was nothing at all actually. We talked about the kids and said goodbye."

Relief flooded through me. "Good. I like to hear that."

It wasn't the first time we'd seen Lila since being together, but it was the first time we'd all been that close together. The town was too small to completely avoid them. I knew that he was over her, but it was good to know that it was all really over. Just me and Ash against the world.

Ash had proposed a few months after the Charleston boutique had opened, and we were married at the start of the next year. We had gotten pregnant with James almost immediately, and it was the best moment of my entire life when Ash held our child for the first time.

"James, don't get ice cream on your suit," Ash said, leaning forward to wipe chocolate off of his suit coat.

The little man was already dressed for Mass, where we'd meet our respective families.

Ash's father had recently passed from a second massive heart attack. Ash had inherited the entire company and fallen into the CEO position, as he'd always been groomed to do. We missed having his father around, but his mom was already dating again. I was happy for her, but Ash thought it was a lot.

"Are you ready for church?" I asked the kids.

They both groaned. Katie liked the singing, but James was too fidgety to sit through most of it. We wouldn't have been going at all if we could have helped it, but I wanted them to grow up just like we had. With Charleston summers, Holy Cross and St. Catherine's schools, and a lifetime of good memories.

I'd opened a store a year the first couple of years after my Charleston location took off. I was already in negotiations to open stores nationwide. That would happen soon enough, but in the meantime, I was focusing on my family.

Ash took my hand, he held James's hand, and I reached for Katie. We walked down Broughton together toward the cathedral. James had a stain on his suit. Katie kept trying to bound ahead and run into traffic like the little Tasmanian devil she was. But it was perfect in its own way.

Our little family.

The dream I'd been following for all these years.

The one that actually came true.

ACKNOWLEDGMENTS

Wait for Always is for the people who "chose the wrong guy." Inevitably there's always someone who loved the other hero in a love triangle and felt broken by the loss. As I dived into Ash's story from the point of view of other characters in the series, I knew there was so much more to this hopeless romantic. And he deserved a love just as beautiful.

So thank you to all the readers who asked for more Ash Talmadge after the ending of *Hold the Forevers*. Especially Anjee Sapp, who was Team Ash from the start!

Special thanks to everyone on my team who helped bring this together: Staci Hart, Devin McCain, Rebecca Kimmerling, Rebecca Gibson, Danielle Sanchez, Ashley Estep, and Kimberly Brower.

As always, my husband Joel and two puppies!

The playlist for this book was primarily: *You Are in Love* by Taylor Swift, *Happier Than Ever* by Kelly Clarkson, *Romantic Disaster* by Lil Lotus, Against the Current, and Chrissy Costanza, Harry's House album by Harry Styles, and *Running Up That Hill* by Kate Bush.

ABOUT THE AUTHOR

 K.A. Linde is the *USA Today* bestselling author of more than thirty novels. She has a Masters degree in political science from the University of Georgia, was the head campaign worker for the 2012 presidential campaign at the University of North Carolina at Chapel Hill, and served as the head coach of the Duke University dance team.

She loves reading fantasy novels, binge-watching Supernatural, traveling to far off destinations, baking insane desserts, and dancing in her spare time.

She currently lives in Lubbock, Texas, with her husband and two super-adorable puppies.

Visit her online: www.kalinde.com

Or Facebook, Instagram & Tiktok: @authorkalinde

For exclusive content, free books, and giveaways every month. www.kalinde.com/subscribe

CPSIA information can be obtained
at www.ICGtesting.com
Printed in the USA
BVHW030026120123
656153BV00015B/115